Dorado Duet

A Will Service Adventure Thriller

Steven Becker

* * *

Join my mailing list

and get a free copy of Wood's Ledge

http://mactravisbooks.com

Chapter 1

The bartender cast a lazy eye my way. Maybe I'm paranoid, but I suspected he was gauging my response to his subterfuge. The Sangrita chaser had done little to soothe the burning in my throat from the shot of tequila. I was far from an aficionado, but the liquor was a lot harsher than I remembered from the label on the bottle he had poured from. He wasn't all that interested, though, as his other eye was glued to a telanovella. The Spanish soap opera played on a small TV. I turned the shot glass upside down, indicating I was finished. It wouldn't matter because there was no way I was going to move him from his perch on a barstool set in front of the only fan in the room.

To say it was hot was an understatement. Hoping to see some ripples that would portend a coming breeze, I looked out at the water, but with no wind to interrupt its perfect surface, it acted as a mirror, making it feel even hotter. The glass-like surface reflected the washed-out color of the buildings, the rundown docks, and the aging boats that made up the waterfront. Finishing the Sangrita, a tomato and orange-spiced chaser, I pulled some peso notes from the stack on the splintered bar and left a generous tip. In my latest line of work, you needed as many friends as you could find. Hoisting my backpack over a shoulder, I got up and left the shack, hoping it would be cooler closer to the water. I was wrong. Walking over to one of the better-maintained shacks, I noticed the sign hanging from a rusted nail on the door to the marina office—*cerrado*—it was closed. With no choice, I sat on a worn stump and waited.

Puerto Chiapas was pretty far off the beaten path, but being the first or last southern port, depending on which way you were traveling, and only sixteen miles from Guatemala, it warranted a customs and immigration official. The main part of town was across the larger basin, leaving the marina by itself, set inland and accessed through a deepwater channel. The outer basin had several concrete piers jutting into the harbor with shrimping and longline fishing boats tied up and a Pemex gas station. It was one of those places, that although small, attracted many cruisers; its one and only calling card was the first—or last—fuel and water in Mexico. These cruisers were not the big-ship, buffet-eating variety, but the smaller sailboats, bought by dreamers up north, deciding this was the most glamorous way to see the world. You could see the world, but it was slow and far from glamorous. Most fell far short of their goals.

The trip south in the fall, known as the Baja Ha-Ha, was a big convoy of about two hundred vessels making the easy trip from San Diego to Cabo San Lucas and then points south. The return trip, called the Baja Bash because of the headwinds and current that made the voyage home a nightmare, had far fewer boats. Instead of dealing with the hard return trip or hiring a skipper to do it for them, the owners either abandoned the boats in a port like this if they had a loan, or sold the boat for pennies on the dollar if they didn't.

That's where I came in. No matter my trade, and I had failed at several, I was a boat bum at heart. The two-thousand-mile trip back, a nightmare for some, was an adventure for me, and I was happy for the bounty once I reached Salvage Solutions.

I had left San Diego on the red-eye the night before, and, after three flights and two hard layovers, I arrived at the airport in nearby Tapachula. Grabbing a cab, I overpaid the driver to wait for me while I shopped for provisions at a local grocery. Showing up at the quiet marina with boxes of food wasn't discreet, but I wasn't trying to be. Sneaking in at night could get me shot.

The driver dropped me at the marina, where I quickly found my commission. The *Nai'a*, a thirty-eight-foot sloop, was tied up in an outside berth. I was drawn to her lines and rigging and made my way past several skinny chickens, piles of fishing gear, and trash to the slip where she was docked. It was the hottest part of the day, driving everyone under the cover of whatever shade or moving air they could find, and I didn't see a soul as I stepped aboard. Setting the box of groceries and my pack down on the deck, I riffled through the pack, looking for the tools that I had purposefully scattered through various compartments.

There were no repo trade schools, forcing me to find my own mentors, and I had paid an old-timer to show me how to pick locks. Besides an irate owner or a corrupt customs official, a simple padlock or cylinder lock on a cabin or passageway door are the only real obstacles to taking a boat. Although most engines require a key to start, hot wiring a boat was much simpler than a car, and, surprisingly, the bigger the boat, the easier.

Using my body, I shielded the lock from anyone looking from shore and started to manipulate the Allen wrench and screwdriver until I felt the pins give and the lock open. Removing it, I opened the door and entered the cabin. I quickly opened the windows and hatches to get some air flowing. Back outside, I put away the tools and waited a few minutes for the interior to cool down. While I waited, I checked the helm. The cockpit was simple and well set up. I could single-hand her easily.

Braving the heat of the cabin, I went in and started poking around the gauges and controls. The batteries still held a charge, but I would conserve their power for when I needed to start the engine. I had to be ready if sailing her out was my only option.

With the batteries on, I checked the gauges. Fuel read half a tank, and the water was almost empty. I could top off the water without raising any interest from the brothers ashore, but buying fuel here was out of the question. Turning off the batteries to conserve whatever charge they still held, I brought the boxes of provisions into the galley and put them away, then I squared away the cabin and went back outside to plan my exit.

This recovery could go two ways, and since I didn't care to be shot at, I chose the path of least resistance, hoping the marina would take my money and let the boat go. Repossessing boats was a tricky and dangerous business. In the States, where the owners were more attached to their possessions, things could get dangerous, but you had the law on your side. Here the boats were abandoned, but dealing with marinas and customs officials could be interesting. "Stealing" a boat in a third-world country could be deadly.

I had fallen into this gig when I was down on my luck, and with no other prospects my ex-girlfriend took pity on me. It was a good thing, because I was out of options. She had taken a job with Salvage Solutions after dumping me for "lack of ambition." I guess she felt guilty and offered me my first gig in Florida. My first repo had gone surprisingly well.

After arriving at the address with no idea what I was doing, I saw the owners leaving their house through the front door with a cab load of suitcases. The boat was tied up to a dock out back, and, with no one home, I walked aboard, started the engines, and collected my first bounty. That didn't mean I had any repo skills, but growing up in the Keys, I had been around boats all my life. I knew engines and sails and could run just about anything, making me a commodity in a business populated more by thugs than skippers.

After a few touch and go operations, I found my niche in foreign recoveries. These boats were abandoned, minimizing the chance of violence and requiring my skill set to get them back to the States. In these scenarios I had two choices: take them outright and make a run for the twelve-mile line where international law took over, hoping I didn't get shot before I got there, or pay someone off and sail away under a white flag. I generally chose the latter.

So, here I was, waiting for the siesta to end. Sitting on a stump shaded by a small palm, I took out a laminated chart from my backpack and studied my options. There were two ways home once I crossed to Cabo San Lucas. The easiest was to play the typical tourist and sail up the coast. There were a half dozen common stops for sailors cruising this route, and I had each marked on the chart. If things went well, this was the best option. I had also drawn on the chart long diagonal lines pointing northwest and then northeast, forty-five degrees to each other, which showed plan B. The tacks were preplanned and brutal, several taking me a thousand miles from land, but I would be far away from any danger except the sea.

Looking around at the other boats in the marina, I saw several twin-engine outboards that could easily catch the slower sailboat if I had to make a run for it. I studied the boats, looking for a radar dome or tower, thankful that none were visible. Once I was over the horizon, I would be in the clear—if I could reach it. Even with the most favorable wind, running under sail and motor together, the *Nai'a* would have a maximum speed of ten knots, and that was with a strong current. The only way out of here was to hope the local authorities were reasonable—meaning corrupt, but not too corrupt.

I sat there, sweating in the shade, when two men walked toward the marina building where the customs office was located. They nodded at each other and entered through adjacent doors. I waited for a few minutes, both gathering my courage and rehearsing my inadequate Spanish. Finally, I stood and walked toward the closest building, opened the door, and entered the marina office.

"*Hola, señor,*" the man said.

I immediately saw a resemblance between him and the bartender. Sliding an official looking paper across the counter, I asked to pay the bill to clear the *Nai'a*. He took the paper, held it like he could read it, set it back down, turned to a desk behind the counter, and started digging through the stack of paperwork on top. I took the paper back and waited.

"*Cuartocientos dolares,*" he said, handing me a piece of paper with some chicken scratch on it.

I looked it over like it mattered, but four hundred dollars was much less than I had figured. Knowing he expected me to barter with him, I came back with three hundred, and after going back and forth a few times, I let him win and settled on three hundred eighty. I dug the money out of the pack and handed it to him.

"*El recibo, por favor,*" I said.

He shrugged his shoulders. I nodded and left the office and walked to the dock. I boarded the sailboat and was just about ready to cast the lines and get out of there when the door next to the marina office opened. The resemblance to the bartender and the man in the marina office was the first thing I noticed; the second was his hand resting on the sidearm holstered on his belt.

With a nod of his head, he summoned me into the customs office. I had little choice and started rehearsing exit strategies as I retraced my steps to the concrete building. This was unusual, but not unexpected. Normally, I would clear customs at my last port of call before leaving the country. This wasn't the first time I had been "taxed" by a local agent, so I complied.

"Passport," he ordered from behind his desk.

I dug in my pack and gave it to him. I had done nothing wrong, at least that I knew of, and even if I had, refusing him was not going to help. Handing it to him, I searched for the words in Spanish to ask what the problem was.

"I see you came into the country today. What is your

business here?" he asked in accented English after thumbing through the pages.

I thought for a second. The paper I had shown his brother in the marina office was the order from Salvage Services in San Diego. It had an embossed logo that made it look official, but I doubted it would work with the customs officer. "I have been hired to take the *Nai'a* back north," I said, giving him the truth with a few omissions.

"Yes. There is the matter of the exit fees, though," he said.

I knew I was being played. I was already low on cash and had to play this carefully. I knew there was a twenty-five-dollar fee, but that was usually paid at the last port in Mexico. I was more than a thousand miles south. But, this was Mexico, and I dug in my backpack for the cash to pay it. "This should cover it and something for your time," I said, offering a hundred dollars.

"Two thousand dollars," he said without blinking. "And I will hold your passport until it is paid."

I had to regroup. This was more than I had or was willing to pay. I had to buy some time. "I paid the marina bill. There should be no problem to stay aboard then," I stated. A hotel was out of my budget.

"Yes, but you must pay the nightly fee," he said, pulling my passport toward him.

I watched my freedom disappear into a locked drawer. Defeated, I stood and left the office. As I walked to the *Nai'a*, I thought through my options, realizing I had none. I rigged a tarp to shade the cockpit and pulled out my charts. There was little detail of the harbor entrance, not unusual here. I had checked several cruiser forums before leaving, and it didn't appear that the tide mattered. The diagonal lines that showed plan B were daunting, but now were the only option. If I could avoid Mexico, I would deal with the passport problem once I got to San Diego. It didn't really matter—I was going tonight, with or without it.

Chapter 2

Sitting under the tarp, waiting for darkness, hoping for some relief from the heat, I had plenty of time to think about how I happened to be here. I tried to sleep, but the heat made it difficult, so I stared at my charts some more, memorizing the lines of latitude I would cross before I executed each tack. I knew from experience that no matter how easy things looked sitting on land, once you were alone on the ocean, everything was harder. Another look at the sky reassured me that, at least until sunrise tomorrow, the weather would hold. A few cumulous clouds floated lazily across the sky, and there was no sign of them developing into the anvil-shaped thunderheads that would bring squalls.

The lack of activity in the marina was reassuring. It was well out of peak cruising season, when the marina and harbor outside the cut would be filled with boats. Thankfully, no one seemed to notice or care that I was there. Hopefully that same attitude would continue tomorrow morning, when the boat and I would be gone.

The only problem I saw with my plan was the difficulty in navigating the marina. The basin appeared to be man-made, wide enough only for its purpose, and well protected. I was not going to attempt to exit under sail, especially in the dark. My plan was to pull out about nine o'clock. Long enough after sunset to use the darkness as cover, and early enough that the motor would not raise any alarms.

I heard activity ashore and peered around the cabin. Both brothers were leaving their respective offices as if on cue. I watched them head up to the bar without a glance in my direction. That was good news; now I just had to wait.

There was some housekeeping to do, and, with the sun low enough in the sky now to provide some relief from the heat, I went below and removed the cover from the engine compartment. The forty-horsepower diesel looked in good condition. It wouldn't be fast, but it should have enough torque to push the boat through whatever conditions I might encounter. I turned back to the storage lockers and found an adequate tool kit, oil, and the replacement filters I needed. Methodically, I replaced the fuel filter, oil filter, and changed the oil, then I brought the oil pan under one of the LED cabin lights to inspect the old lubricant. It was free of the metal shavings or water that would indicate a problem. I was also relieved to find no water in the fuel separator. Replacing the cover, I cleaned the deck and went topside.

It was dark now, and my watch showed almost eight o'clock. Curious as to what the brothers were up to, I made a few sandwiches, stashing two for later and took one on deck. The marina was mostly dark, but there was still a glow from the shack the bar was in. Not sure whether to worry about them or not, I prepared the boat for sea.

There was nothing to do now except leave. The light was still on in the shack. After two hours of drinking, I hoped the brothers' senses would at least be dulled. Below, I closed the hatches and turned on the batteries. They both showed less than twelve volts, so I turned the switch to *all,* allowing them to work in parallel to start the engine. Back on deck, I went to the helm and held my breath while I pushed the *start* button. The engine caught after two tries, and I looked around to see if anyone noticed. There was always the chance they thought I was running the engine to charge the batteries and would ignore it, but that was not the way my luck usually ran.

This time it appeared to be holding, and after a few minutes of idling, there was still no activity. Leaving the shifter in neutral, I hopped onto the dock and released the lines. Whether they belonged to the boat or to the marina, I took them, needing all the rigging I could get my hands on. Tossing them below, I waited for the tide to move the boat away from the dock and shifted into reverse, almost jumping when the transmission clanked loudly in protest.

There was still no sign I had been observed, or if I had, that anyone cared. Still idling, I let the boat slide backward past the last piling and, once clear, I pushed the lever forward. After another loud clank, the boat inched forward. The tide was mellow, but a gust of wind came up and tried to turn the bow, forcing me to increase RPMs. All of a sudden, the door to the shack opened, and I heard voices in the night.

There was no point in continuing my attempt at subterfuge, and I pushed the throttle down. The boat reacted and quickly moved past the end of the dock. I turned to port and entered the cut between the marina and the larger basin. The engine noise echoed in the tree-lined channel, and several times I thought I heard another boat behind me, but each time I turned to check, I saw nothing.

After a few long minutes, I entered the commercial basin. There was more activity here, especially at the Pemex gas station, which, I regretted, I could not risk visiting. The docks were well lit, and there were fishermen working on nets and drinking beer, but no one seemed to pay me any attention. I continued motoring toward the inlet.

Open water lay in front of me, and I relaxed slightly. If they wanted to catch me, at least for the next few miles there was nothing I could do to counter the speed of the twin outboards in the marina. I expected if they did come, they would search up and down the coast. I held my course due west into open water. I had no plans on seeing anything but the faint outline of land until I reached San Diego.

I had just cleared the inlet when I heard the roar of an outboard. There had been little breeze inside the harbor, but I could feel fifteen knots on my face now and good-sized swells beneath my feet. Setting the autopilot to a north-northwest course into the wind, I ran forward and hauled up the mainsail. If I had thought about it, I might have put a reef in the sail, knowing from experience that the wind was likely to pick up as I got offshore. Right now, I needed all the speed I could get and ran back to the cockpit, where I cranked the winch until the sail was fully raised.

Taking control back from the autopilot, I steered a westerly course to gain as much speed as possible. The boat heeled over and I could hear the water rushing beneath the hull. After trimming the main sheet, I reached over and unfurled the jib. With both sails and the motor, the speed indicator showed nine knots. It was not enough to outrun the outboard I suspected was after me, but if I could just get over the dark horizon, I would be invisible.

The lights from the town were receding behind me when I saw red and green dots coming directly toward me. The outboard had cleared the inlet, and I thought for a minute that they had seen me. Then, I could only see the green light and breathed a sigh of relief. They had apparently chosen to follow the coast to the north. I worked the sails to coax as much speed as I could get from her and smiled as the *Nai'a* crashed through the swells.

About what I guessed was a mile from the inlet, the waves doubled in height, and I looked behind me to see the town disappear behind the wall of water. I was grateful for the big seas; the height of the waves would help camouflage me, and I doubted the brothers would follow in these conditions. Focusing on the boat and rigging, I regretted not putting the reef in the sail. It was too rough to chance a trip to the foredeck to do it now, but I could furl the jib from the cockpit. I reached behind me, took a turn of the free line around the cleat, and pulled the line to the roller furling. The wind had a hold of the sail and fought against my efforts, forcing me to either bear off or use the winch to bring in some of the sail. I chose the winch. There was no way I was giving ground so close to freedom.

When I had a third of the jib in, the boat settled, and I looked back at the vacant sea. A few twinkles of light from the taller buildings in town were visible when I crested a wave, but there was no sign of any navigation lights.

I was alone with a good boat—a good place for me.

Chapter 3

I was close enough to see the smoke rings from his cigar before they dispersed. The humid tropical air was thick and they floated slowly toward the sky. I was that close. And it wouldn't have mattered if I were sitting on his lap, like the topless bimbo currently squirming there—he wasn't the kind of guy that noticed people like me. The wind had dropped and the sun was about four fingers from the horizon when I turned away from the sixty-eight-foot sportfisher *Dorado* and went to the helm of the *Nai'a*.

The thirty-eight-foot sailboat and I had gone round a few times since leaving Puerto Chiapas under cover of darkness. After our escape, a few hundred miles sailing into the wind had been our rocky courtship, but we had moved on and were into our honeymoon phase. I'd fought her and she had fought back, and like every successful relationship, somewhere along the way we had earned each other's respect and learned to live with each other's faults. The one thing I had to admit was that I had far more than the cruiser.

But the plan didn't stay the plan for very long. I was well offshore when the wind changed and the storm came up, forcing me to lower sail and power for endless hours through two-story-high waves. Worn out and with fuel, water, and provisions running low, I changed course for Cabo San Lucas. I expected the tourist port to be busy enough to allow me to anchor off the beach and use the dinghy to shuttle fuel and water back and forth without having to clear customs and immigration or be asked to show my nonexistent passport.

The storm had blown out, but it left me well short of my destination. The northwest winds resumed, and, with the cross-track error on the GPS set to five miles, I zigzagged, tacking every hour or so to maintain the most direct course I could manage to reach the southern end of Baja Peninsula.

The lights from the tourist district guided me past the point, and I could see the famous sea arch that marked the intersection of the Pacific Ocean and the Sea of Cortez, backlit by the moon. I looked for a safe spot outside of the harbor to anchor and get some much-needed sleep. Five sleepless days after leaving Puerto Chiapas, I dropped sail in the protected waters past Lovers Beach, tossed the anchor, and called it a night.

In the morning, feeling refreshed, I loaded the gas cans into the dinghy, calculating it would take two trips to top the tanks. By noon I should be fueled, watered, and provisioned, and, with any luck, I would be into blue water by sunset. I had just started out for the harbor when my phone dinged with an offer I couldn't refuse.

* * *

It was easy to locate the target. Marinetraffic.com showed the position of every vessel on the water anywhere in the world that had a transponder aboard and, whether the owners knew it or not, every vessel that had a lien on its title had one. I pulled out my phone, opened the Internet browser, and entered the website name. Several icons appeared by my location, including mine, which set me back several minutes as I located the small device in a panel behind the VHF radio and removed the power harness. I sat on the settee rereading the text from Salvage Solutions, went back to the browser, and located the boat in question.

The *Dorado* was two miles away, off the beach, on the other side of the harbor. After my second trip, I stowed the provisions, topped off the tanks, pulled anchor, and motored to a spot about fifty feet away from the large sportfisher in thirty feet of water off Playa El Médano. Set among a slew of private and charter boats, with snorkelers diving on the reef below, I wasn't worried about being noticed and dropped anchor.

I had no plan other than to observe. Sitting in the cockpit, I watched as another smoke ring drifted across my rail, and I heard several women giggle. Another pair were in the water snorkeling off the stern of the boat. Moving forward for a better view, I went to the bow, tidied some lines and decided to let some more anchor line out to counter the afternoon breeze that had started to kick up whitecaps. All the while, I watched the cockpit of the boat in front of me. The sun was almost down, and the party was getting louder.

"Hey, sport. You a little close?"

The voice startled me, and I looked up to see a shotgun barrel extending from the bridge, pointing in my direction. I looked around and realized most of the other boats had gone in for the day. We were the only two left—so much for not being noticed. I nodded, went to the helm, and started the engine. In neutral, I revved the engine to twenty-five hundred RPMs and hit the windlass switch. The anchor was so light it barely put a strain on the motor, and the line and chain were quickly aboard. Setting the engine back to idle, I ran forward to secure the anchor when I heard the first shots.

I dropped back, using the mast as cover, and hauled hard on the halyard. Fortunately, the current was strong, and the boat had swung beam to the waves, giving the man on the flybridge of the sportfisher a bad angle—at least for now. I heard the whine of the larger boat's windlass, and knew I was in trouble. The halyard came free, and I ran back to the cockpit and pulled on the line. The mainsail rose slowly, until three-quarters of the way up it resisted my efforts. It would take the winch from here—something I had no time for. Locking the line, I ran back to the helm, pushed the throttle forward and spun the wheel to starboard. The bow slammed into a wave, throwing spray back toward me, but I ignored it and held course. With a slam, the boom swung over and the sail caught the wind. The *Nai'a* jumped, showing the speed and grace of the dolphin she was named for.

I could hear orders being given aboard *Dorado*. With the sail up, I could no longer see the activity on deck, and my gut tightened when I heard the big diesels roar to life. I shifted my focus from the other boat; I needed to concentrate on my end of things if I was going to get out of this. Engaging the autopilot to keep the sails on a close reach, her fastest point of sail, I leaned over the rail and released the jib furling. The foresail caught instantly, and the boat gained speed.

Chancing a look back, I saw the bow of the sportfisher turn toward me and another shot fired. I was making close to ten knots now and had the winch in my hand, ready to trim the sails, when I saw the big boat jerk forward and kick a huge bow wake. Just as I had *Nai'a* trimmed, the sportfisher spun and headed to the harbor. I hadn't had time to analyze their motives, but I doubted they had suspected my intentions. Fueled by alcohol, they were just throwing their weight around for the amusement of a few bar girls. I held course, putting as much space between us as I could if he decided to come back. At the same time, knowing that I was under armed and underpowered, a confrontation would not work out well for me.

In the dying light, I watched the boat slow and enter the harbor. Relieved, I cut the wheel to starboard and brought the bow of the *Nai'a* through the wind. The sails swung over, the main needed no adjustment, but the jib was hove to, blocking the wind from the mainsail and slowing the boat. Setting the autopilot, I worked the lines, easing the sails before once again taking control of the boat. I worked her to a broad reach and went to the chart plotter, thinking I had better get some information on who was aboard before I went any further with this contract.

* * *

Sheryl had been on the other end of the line when I answered the phone earlier, offering me one of those life-changing deals. Now, after doing a little research, the deal didn't seem quite as sweet—only the small matter of repossessing a million-dollar sportfisher from a known gangster stood in the way of a six-figure payday. It was worth thinking about. With that kind of money, I could make one trip a year down south, and, instead of repossessing boats, actually buy the ones owned outright for pennies on the dollar, sail them north, and more than double my money, all the while living large on a beautiful cruiser.

A quick Google search with the name of the boat had given me more information than I wanted. The owner, Sam Chuy, was West Coast mob. The son of Joey Chuy, the man who, with his unique mix of Italian and Japanese bloodlines, had united the warring families in L.A. into a criminal empire. The apple fell close to the tree, then rolled downhill and never stopped. Sam was now estranged from the family and in deep debt. Rumor had it there was a seven-figure contract on him. With his boat and whatever assets he could get his hands on, he'd fled L.A. Now the bank wanted the boat back.

Cabo was convenient, and Chuy was no rocket scientist. The radar transponder was still active, allowing me to use my phone and a half dozen clicks to find him. Now all I had to do was wrestle a million-dollar boat away from a mobster.

The boat disappeared around a bend in the harbor, and I turned a few degrees into the wind to find an anchorage. There was little in the way of protected water on the coast, so I settled on a sandy spot a few hundred yards from the beach. Despite the earlier weather, the wind typically died at night, and the waves were already subsiding with the sunset. Spinning the wheel to point the bow to the wind, I dropped into neutral and released the halyard, allowing the mainsail to drop into its lazy jacks. Moving to the port rail, I released the tension on the jib sheet and pulled the furling line until the jib was wrapped neatly around the forestay.

The anchor dropped and I backed down on the hook, paying out all the line the locker held. I could feel the grab and shut down the engine. Normally this was rum-thirty, but not tonight—I was going to town.

Chapter 4

Running the engine had not only given me more speed, but had a nice side benefit—hot water. The crescent moon reflecting on the surface of the still water cast a dim light, allowing me to shower on the swim platform. It was the only way I could clean up aboard a boat. Even built like a cornerback, I had no idea how a linebacker could fit into the tight head. I ran my hands across my face to check for any spots that I had missed while shaving and did a little cleanup. After drying off, I changed into my traveling clothes: a button-down short sleeve shirt, and cargo shorts. It had been so long since I had worn shoes that even the flip-flops felt uncomfortable.

I pulled the painter in and climbed aboard the dinghy, started the engine, and steered a course parallel to the coast. The ride to the harbor was longer than I would have liked. I would have preferred a beach landing, but the sound of surf crashing on the sand made me wary. Instead, I stayed a hundred yards offshore and kept the speed low enough to remain dry. Pointed directly between the jetties, I idled toward the harbor entrance. Once inside the breakwater, I eased off the throttle and started cruising the docks. With water taxis running back and forth between the resorts and restaurants, there was enough boat traffic that my dinghy remained inconspicuous. It wasn't as busy as during the day, when the same taxis shuttled tourists to Lovers Beach or El Arco and snorkeling and sportfishing charters were active. I must have blended in pretty well because the lone police cruiser I saw ignored me.

Docks were everywhere, with all manner of craft tied up in the slips. The piers were lettered, and I followed along, starting with A on the northeastern end and moving through the alphabet. I turned at D dock, reversing course, still watching for the *Dorado*. In many harbors she would have stuck out, but not here. Finally, I found the sportfisher tucked behind the municipal pier. With the throttle set at a low idle, I steered toward her. Using the structure for cover, I slid within a hundred feet of the *Dorado*. The boat was quiet now, with only two LED lights illuminating the rear deck. There were lights below in the fore and aft cabins, dashing my dreams of an easy repo. I had to assume Chuy, the captain, or the man who had shot at me earlier was aboard, and knowing they had weapons changed my thought process.

I followed the dock to the seawall, surveying each slip as I passed. Finally, I found a boat that was shut up tight. There was no indication of anyone currently residing on her, and I took a chance and tied off the dinghy to the aft cleat and climbed over the transom. The trawler shifted slightly with my weight, and I stood still for a long minute, waiting for it to settle. Reassured that she was vacant, I stealthily crept across the deck to the rail and climbed onto the dock. Again, I waited to make sure no one had seen me.

From the look of things, Chuy and his entourage had either gone to town, or the party had moved below decks. The dock provided little cover, just a six-foot-wide walkway with finger piers running off it. It was about three-quarters full, leaving enough gaps between the boats that I felt very exposed. As far as I knew, no one knew me, which was both good and bad. On some docks a stranger stands out, on others they blend in, and I had no idea which one I was on. The boats, expensive sportfishers, convertibles, and sailboats, were all large enough to live aboard, and many had a steady stream of water discharging into the harbor, indicating their air conditioning was running. Fortunately, it was still hot, keeping the occupants below deck, but it was almost too quiet.

Water misted down from the stainless-steel tower of one of the larger sportfishers, and I looked up to see several deckhands cleaning and buffing the tall structure. Moving toward Chuy's boat, I stayed to the far side of the dock, as if I had business with one of the boats docked there. I walked toward the end of the pier, passing the *Dorado*, then turned and walked back, slower this time. The light was still on below, and I thought I saw the shadow of someone moving in the cabin when I heard a muffled cry. At first I thought it was one of the feral cats common to most marinas and continued walking until, I heard it again.

Instinctively I turned and recognized it as human, female, and being kept against its will. Then it was quiet—too quiet—and I realized I had not seen anyone, either on the dock or on the decks of any of the boats. Chuy's reputation must have preceded him, and they were all just killing time in town or below decks until he was gone.

I was faced with one of those decisions that I am not very good at making. At this point I was not involved, and I could walk away if I chose. The only problem was that I never choose to walk away. Saying yes had been a problem from my days as a carpenter and fishing guide. Yes, I can install a custom trim package for clients on a ridiculous budget. Yes, we can go out, knowing full well that the fishing was going to be bad and the client, although they said they would be happy just to get out and toss a line, wouldn't be. That one word killed my reputation when jobs came in behind schedule and over budget, or clients came back to the dock with no fish—and it was even worse when women were involved.

Yes was the answer again. The lure of the immense payday

and the mystery of the woman aboard had my senses heightened, and I could feel the blood pounding in my ears. As Watson said to Holmes: *The game's afoot.* Yes made me a different person. It gave me an edge and a reason. It wasn't the money, recognition, or achievements that got the adrenaline pumping, it was doing something that other people couldn't or wouldn't do.

I looked around the dock. I needed to get low without attracting attention to myself. The dinghy was not an option; its tin can engine made too much noise, and whoever was onboard would surely take notice and investigate. The slip to the right was empty; the one to the left had a nice sailboat. I went toward it.

It's not hard to tell when a boat is occupied or not. First, there was no water spouting from the outlet, and the hatches were closed. Closed up like that without air conditioning, it would be a sauna. Two bicycles were leaned together, chained and locked to the wire safety rail. The canvas was rolled up, safely protected from the elements in zippered cocoons. No, without AC or shade, the boat was empty.

There was an opening in the safety rail about halfway down the starboard side finger pier, but in order to reach it I would have to pass the lit cabin window on Chuy's boat. The port side pier was shared with another boat that had the flash of a TV screen coming from its sliding glass door. I hesitated, not totally trusting my knee, and vaulted the railing on the transom. Landing in a crouch, I froze for an instant and, when nothing moved around me, went forward to the passageway.

I used the narrow alcove for cover and looked back at the sportfisher. Leaning against the locked cabin door, I waited, listening and watching the larger boat. Scenarios started to run through my mind as I waited: knock out whoever was aboard, rescue the girl, and motor out of here with my big payday was the most popular. Several others did not have such a happy ending, and I started to get second thoughts.

The alcove leading to the cabin below concealed me, but it also hid most of Chuy's boat. The constant flow of water from the air conditioning system also covered all but the loudest of sounds. If I wanted scenario number one to work, I had to move. Looking around, my attention was drawn to the flybridge on an equally impressive sportfisher that had backed into the slip across from Chuy's. The ladder to access the bridge was off the aft deck, but each corner of the structure was a lattice of stainless steel tubing. *Dorado* would likely have the same structure, and if I could reach the corner adjacent to the finger pier without being seen, I could climb it.

Looking both ways, I waited until I was sure no one was coming and made my move. Planning my landing before my feet left the ground, I sprang from the passageway and ran to the transom of the sailboat. I was airborne, flying toward the sportfisher. Then a thin piece of stainless wire that ran around the top of the safety rail—and invisible in the dark—snagged my foot, and I started to fall. It played out in slow motion, and I knew from other injuries that when things started to slow down it was going to be bad. Maybe if I had ditched my flip-flops I could have made it, but I hadn't. The wire caught between the thin rubber sole and my toes, pushing me forward without releasing me. The seawall passed in front of my face, and I hung in space for a long second before the rubber sole broke and I crashed into the water.

I flailed in the tepid water. Reaching for the surface, my hand found a line and instinctively I pulled on it. Holding on to the thick rope, I held my head above the waterline and sucked in air, trying to catch my breath. It took a minute to regain my bearings. The tide this close to the equator doesn't fluctuate more than a foot, but it was low now, and that foot kept the dock above my head just out of reach. The sailboat I had jumped from had an enclosed transom and no swim ladder. My only way back onto the dock was the line in my hands.

I started climbing hand over hand, struggling until my feet were out of the water and able to assist. First one hand hit the weathered wood and then the other. I took a deep breath and hauled myself onto the small finger pier and collapsed. Swearing to myself that I would start working out tomorrow, I got to my knees. With one hand on a piling, I was about to gain my feet when I heard the cabin door on Chuy's boat open and then the unmistakable sound of a shotgun being cocked. I froze in place and our eyes met.

Refocusing from the end of the barrel to the man behind the trigger, the first thing I noticed was the almond tilt to his eyes, then the stubble on his chin and the cigar butt in his mouth. I knew I was looking at Sam Chuy. I scrapped scenario number one.

Chapter 5

Scenario number two was now top priority—run. Run fast, run hard, and don't look back. With my one remaining flip-flop in hand, I swam the length of the dock to the sailboat my dinghy was tied to. I risked a look behind, but the dock was empty. Chuy must have gone back inside, thinking me an idiot and not a threat. That was fine with me, because right now, that was what I was thinking of myself.

I reached the dinghy and swung myself aboard, tossing the lone flip-flop in before me. The fuel line had held its prime, and the engine started on the first pull. Releasing the painter, I started to gun the throttle to get out of the harbor faster, but thought better of it when I approached Chuy's boat, and I slowed to a low idle. Coasting by the bow of the sportfisher, I was sure I heard the same whimper as before. For a brief second I subconsciously veered toward the boat, like there was really something I could do to help whoever was aboard. I caught myself and turned toward the main channel. The last thing I wanted was to be staring into the barrel of that shotgun again.

As I steered toward the moonlight-dappled water of the Sea of Cortez, I hoped Chuy was thinking that the whole incident was insignificant, that I was just a fly buzzing around. Being seen had not been on my agenda, and now I was forced to regroup and rethink my strategy. A single sighting was one thing, but recognizing me again would surely set off alarms. Twice the shotgun had been pointed at me. I wasn't eager for a third try.

I crossed the narrow part of the channel. Staying close to the north shore, I passed a long commercial pier and then several boats moored nose in and perpendicular to the rocky shore. I heard the roar of an outboard engine approaching the inlet, and, realizing I had no navigation lights, I stayed as close to the boats as I could. The twin-engine cigarette boat cruised in and slowed, catching me in its wake as it settled to an idle and entered the harbor. The wake was pushing me back into the moored boats. Cursing the boat, I gunned the engine several times to power through. Finally, the last wave passed, and I steered toward the small rocky point marking the entrance. Once around it, I followed the beach to where the *Nai'a* was anchored.

Something was wrong. I thought I might have missed my landmarks, so I continued along the moonlit beach. Several boats were swinging on anchors or moorings, but none was mine. I turned when I heard waves crashing on the rocks, and in the moonlight I saw the beach ended just ahead. Following the same course back, I motored to where I remembered anchoring, but there was nothing but water.

I cut the engine and drifted. Moonlight penetrated the first few feet of water, revealing nothing and quickly fading to black. Looking back up, I scanned the surface of the water and then the surrounding boats. Nothing. I had worried earlier about how I was going to handle two boats by myself. Now I had none—*Nai'a* had either sunk or had been taken.

I was out of scenarios now, having exhausted the only ones that had come to mind. Sitting out here was not going to accomplish anything, so I pulled the starter rope. Thankfully something went right and the engine caught. Now I had to decide where to go. The main harbor at Cabo was out of bounds. I had a few wet dollars in my pocket, one shoe, and my going-to-town clothes were soaking wet. If Chuy didn't find me, I would be a magnet for the local police.

San José del Cabo was more laid back and would be more receptive. I shook the five-gallon gas can with my foot, cursing myself for not bringing extra. There were no more than two gallons left, not enough for the twenty-mile trip up the coast. My attention turned toward the beach. It would be an easy landing, but was heavily patrolled by security guards employed by the side-by-side resorts to keep trash like me out. The harbor seemed the only alternative.

I motored back to the rock jetty and followed the gravel beach back to the first dock. Chuy's boat was directly across from me, with lights shining from every hatch and porthole. Moving further into the harbor seemed like a bad idea. I changed course and gunned the motor to cross the narrow inlet. The docks on the southern side were mostly empty, their exposure to the open water making them less desirable. I pulled into the far slip, tied the dinghy to a pile and sat there.

After a few minutes of feeling sorry for myself, I took inventory. Emptying my pockets produced a ruined phone, about fifty dollars in wet bills, and my rigging knife. Not one to remain morose, I jammed everything back into my pockets, hopped onto the dock, and started walking.

The first thing I needed was footwear. My clothes were almost dry from the boat ride, but my feet were stinging from the pebbles scattered on the uneven pavement. Turning into the first T-shirt shop I saw, I bought a pair of the cheapest flip-flops they had, immediately grateful for the relief when I put them on. On the way out, I used the mirror of a sunglasses display and combed my hair with my hands.

Outside, I looked around. Bars and restaurants beckoned from every angle, but I avoided them and turned toward the masts in the harbor. It was a long walk around, but the *Nai'a* might be there. If not, she was up in San José or long gone. If I found her, I would have another set of problems: the letter of authority to repossess her was aboard the boat. I had no legal claim without it. Of course, a copy was on my phone, but that was now useless.

I passed the pier where Chuy's boat was tied up without incident and continued on to the other alphabet labeled docks. None of the sailboats caught my eye, and I was halfway around the marina when I got the feeling I was being followed.

"Turn right onto the next dock," a man's voice said from behind me.

My first instinct was to look back, but I resisted. I knew he was talking to me. At P dock I turned as instructed. I was getting worried, and nervously fondled the rigging tool in my pocket, wondering if the marlinspike would be useful as a weapon.

"Don't worry. I mean no harm," the voice reassured me in heavily accented English.

With little choice, I followed the dock. A hand suddenly reached out behind me and guided me to the same twin-engine cigarette boat that had almost dumped me earlier. I was ushered aboard, and another man came out of the shadows, edged close to me, but turned away and released the lines.

"Will Service. My name is Ramon. We have something in common," he said, starting one engine at a time and pulling forward into the channel.

I studied the man at the helm. He was well groomed, with neatly trimmed salt and pepper hair, dressed in a polo shirt and khaki shorts. Not the kind of guy you'd expect to follow you, he looked more like he was on vacation from Wall Street. "What can I do for you?"

"It's more like what we can do together," he said, skillfully guiding the boat through the cut.

Without a word, he pushed the throttles forward, and I grabbed the tubing at the side of the leaning post as the boat jumped onto plane and sped north. It was too loud to talk, so I hung on and waited. I've been around boats for a long time and was pretty good at estimating speed and distance. We were running a bit over forty knots, and when we turned to port, passing a long breakwater and entered another inlet, I suspected we were in San José. He slowed and entered the harbor.

San José had a reputation for being the laid-back version of Cabo, and the harbor lived up to that expectation. It was smaller, the boats were smaller, and the nightlife was quiet. Ramon stayed to the southern docks, stopped and backed skillfully into a slip. The other man aboard took care of the lines, and we stepped onto the dock.

"Coffee?" Ramon asked.

"I'd rather a beer," I said. I was already amped up. He led me down the street to a small bar. We entered and took seats in a quiet booth near the back.

"Sam Chuy," he said, looking for recognition on my face. "You've been following him."

There was no reason to dispute what he already knew. "Right. I have a contract to repossess his boat."

"We are not here to stand in your way, but there is something aboard that we must have before you take the vessel," he said.

The waitress interrupted the conversation, setting our two beers in front of us.

"Something—or someone?" I said before I could stop myself.

He rubbed his clean-shaven face and brushed his hands back through his hair. "All right. Someone."

The pieces were falling together now. "And my boat, the *Nai'a*?"

"We will return the boat if you cooperate with us," he said, his veneer breaking slightly.

"Why do you need me?" I was always skeptical when

someone used "we" so freely.

"We need an outsider. Someone Chuy will not suspect," he said. "Someone who knows boats and the water."

I sipped my beer and thought for a minute. This guy was no gangster. I was sure from his demeanor and accent that he had at least gone to school in the States. He was as nervous as I was. "You've got to level with me."

It was his turn to sit and think. Finally he signaled for two more beers. "Do you know who Gerardo is?"

I shook my head.

"He is the captain of the Mexican National Soccer team. Very famous player."

"Okay." Despite spending too many Sundays on the water, I followed American football—soccer was lost on me.

"Chuy has kidnapped my sister, Gerardo's girlfriend."

The beers arrived just in time to give me a few minutes to figure out how big the pile of crap I had just stepped into really was. He obviously didn't have enough *we's* to follow me earlier and know that Chuy had seen me. "Just pay someone."

He sipped his beer and looked at me. "We will give you all the help you need."

Chapter 6

I had nowhere else to go and had to at least find out where he had stashed the *Nai'a*. There was no need for a blindfold as we followed the dark winding roads into the desert hills above Cabo San José. A low line of clouds had slid in from the north, dissipating the moonlight and giving the landscape an eerie glow. We had left town in an SUV driven by the nameless man from the boat. From his lack of speech, I assumed he was Ramon's bodyguard. At first I thought this was superfluous, but after we left Route 10 and entered the hill country, I was happy for his presence. This was exactly the kind of area that gringos were not supposed to frequent at night. After leaving the paved highway, the only thing I could see was the gravel road lit by the bouncing headlights. We followed the potholed road as it climbed into the hills, winding around sharp switchbacks to handle the steep grade.

We stopped a half a bone-jarring hour later. It took a few minutes for the dust to settle before I saw the ranch gate blocking the road. The driver went to open the gate.

"We should be there in a few minutes," Ramon said.

I looked around at the landscape illuminated by the SUV's headlights. It was barren. "Where exactly is here?" I asked.

"Gerardo's ranch," he said. "You will be safe here tonight."

Safe? I thought. I wasn't sure I had any imminent threats. Chuy had seen me, but he had no idea who I was. "Safe from what?"

The driver was back, and Ramon turned to face the road as we entered the property. He remained silent when the driver stopped on the other side to close the gate. The road was better now; it had been machine graded, as if someone cared about it. Private money versus public money in Mexico made all the difference. In the moonlight I could see scrawny cattle standing by the barbwire fence, and soon there was a blur of light ahead. As we approached the house, my interest in carpentry and architecture overcame my wariness. I studied the building and grounds with a tradesman's eye.

The ranch-style house was well proportioned with welcoming patios on the three sides of the building visible from the driveway. Hand-scraped logs were used for columns, enhancing the rustic look, and the stucco was artfully done to look like adobe plaster. Generous roof overhangs supported by wooden corbels accented mahogany windows and doors. Warm light shone through the front windows, lending a welcoming glow to the house. The landscaping belied the region with a lush lawn and plenty of foliage, also well lit.

"You appreciate the details," Ramon said as we entered the two-story foyer.

"I was a carpenter in a past life," I said, now freely looking at the interior detailing. The mahogany trim was recessed into the plaster, giving the house an old-world appearance. The exposed beams and hand-scraped wood floor finished the look. "It is well done."

"Would you like to get some rest, or would you rather talk now?" he asked.

There was no chance for sleep until I got some answers. "Now, if you don't mind."

He led me down a wide hallway past a kitchen on one side and a dining room on the other to a large pair of arched carved doors. The backyard was like a resort, capped off with a meandering infinity edged pool. We walked to a pergola with a table and chairs underneath. He motioned me to a seat. After retrieving two cold beers from a refrigerator behind a bar, he sat across from me.

"As I said before, we have a common interest in Chuy."

My bottle burst just as I put it to my mouth, and a stream of gunfire erupted. Instinctively I ducked below the table and flattened myself on the flagstone patio. Suddenly it was quiet, and I looked around for Ramon. He was still sitting, and I wondered why he hadn't taken cover when I saw the pool of blood forming by his feet. More shots fired from the house, and I heard the bodyguard call out my name.

I started to move toward the voice, but the shooters must have seen the movement and started firing again. Another round came from behind me, closer this time.

"Crawl to the doors. I'll cover you," the man yelled over the gunfire.

I was frozen in place, scared to move, when something exploded by the bar. Whoever was out there was not taking prisoners. Some ancient survival instinct took hold, and I started crawling to the house. Several bursts of gunfire came from the opened door, quelling the other shooters enough for me to make the threshold.

"Follow me," the man ordered.

He led me to a side door. "What about the SUV?" I asked.

"They'll have someone watching," he said, looking both ways before hunching over and running a serpentine course toward the brush.

With no choice, I followed, mimicking his movements. We were clear of the house, and the gunfire had stopped. I could hear my heart beat in my ears as I followed the bodyguard into the unknown. The brush opened up to a small clearing with a barn.

The man stopped at the last tree and waited. He looked around and, with his rifle braced against his shoulder, was ready to shoot. It seemed deserted, and he started for the barn. We made the doors and he reached into his pocket for a key chain. Handing me a single key, he nodded to the lock, turned his back to me, and scanned the surroundings.

My hands were sweaty, and my heart was beating fast. I fumbled with the lock, but, finally, the key slid in and turned. With the door cracked, I slid in just as bullets struck around me and gunfire echoed in my ears. I stood frozen, waiting for the bodyguard to return fire, when I heard a body fall to the ground. The man lay in the doorway. I leaned over and saw blood pouring out of a chest wound and starting to trickle out of his mouth.

Suddenly he reached up and grabbed me, pulling me to his face. With the smell of death on his breath, he said, "Marcella."

His hand dropped, and I knew without checking that he was dead. I remained in a crouch. The shots were coming in bursts of two or three, and I heard voices outside. My eyes had adjusted to the darkness, and I looked around. A tractor was behind me. Grabbing the man's gun, I started to move toward the protection of the steel bucket when I had an idea. Quickly searching him, I found a wallet and a cell phone. I stuffed them in my pockets

I scrambled behind the bucket and set the barrel of the rifle on the edge, aiming at the door. The voices were closer now, and I could hear footsteps approaching. They must have seen the bodyguard go down. I waited for the showdown, glancing around to see if there was a back door, when I saw the outline of a vehicle under a tarp. Just then, the door opened, and I ran for it.

The tarp came off just as the first bullet struck the bucket, and the beam of a powerful flashlight penetrated the darkness. The old Jeep looked like it had seen better days, but the key was in the ignition, and I was out of options. The light hit me, and I heard the men shouting. Holding my breath, I turned the key. The starter turned, but the engine didn't catch. A bullet hit the old leather headrest, missing me by inches, and I leaned forward and tried again. This time it caught.

My foot found the clutch, and I rammed the stick into first gear. With a jolt, the car lurched forward, but before it could stall, I found the clutch, depressed it slightly, and hit the gas pedal with my other foot. Surprised by the power, I was out of the barn in seconds, blazing down an old gravel road. Shots came from behind, taking out the rear window when the first turn took me by surprise, and I ran off the road. Gravel flew from the wheels as I struggled with the steering wheel, finally gaining control and pulling the car back on the road.

I risked a glance in the rearview window after the next hard turn and slowed. The barn was out of sight, and there was no one behind me. Focusing on the road, I accelerated, taking the turns like a NASCAR driver. When I was sure no one was following, I slowed, pulled off to the side and, with a tinge of paranoia that it wouldn't start again, killed the engine and headlights.

I sat in the dark, surrounded by silence, stars, and the dessert. I slumped over the wheel and waited, jumping at every sound, but there was nothing man-made. After a while, how long I'm not really sure, my heartbeat settled and I started to think clearly. Starting with the first shots, I pieced together what had happened, looking for any clue that might help me survive. I didn't know who was out there, but their intentions were clear.

I came away with only one thing: the girl being held on Chuy's boat and the *Nai'a* were linked together. I wasn't sure if the money was worth my life, and the thought occurred to me that I could drive the Jeep to the border and be back in L.A. by this time tomorrow. But then reality set in. I had no passport and little money. I had lost the *Nai'a*, and Chuy knew what I looked like. This was bad.

My mind worked through every possible solution. Walking

into the US Embassy with a concocted story about a stolen passport seemed to be the best option. It might get me back into the States, but my reputation, or what was left of it, would be ruined. There was also a good chance the customs official who had taken my passport had put out an alert that would land me in a third-world jail. Scrapping that idea, I thought about the girl on the boat and the name Marcella.

Chapter 7

I jumped when the first rays of the sun hit me, wondering where I had awoken. The scene in front of me was surreal; the pink light from the sunrise turned to a vibrant crimson when it reached the line of clouds over the mist-covered water. Below me the small town of Cabo San José, still in shadows, twinkled like a Christmas tree. To each side, the foothills extended to the water. It was not at all congruent to the desert scene around me.

Slowly, I went through my body, stiff from sleeping in the car. I appeared uninjured and opened the door to stretch my legs. My situation didn't look as bleak in the daylight as it had in darkness. It looked like I had escaped or rather temporarily evaded whoever had killed Ramon and the bodyguard last night. If I could only find the *Nai'a*, I could forget about Chuy and the woman, turn the bow south, round the point of Cabo San Lucas, and cruise up the coast to L.A.

I went back to the Jeep, thinking that was my best option, and sat behind the wheel wondering where to start my search when I felt a vibration in my pocket. The phone I had taken from the bodyguard buzzed again and I removed it. *Marcella* flashed on the screen, and I remembered the name whispered by the man as he died.

I thought about answering, but wasn't bold enough. Instead, I sat in the worn leather seat with the phone in my lap, staring at the screen. The call ended, and it went black, but came to life a second later with a message in Spanish, which I assumed indicated a new voicemail. I could ignore it, but there was no harm in opening it. I felt more comfortable without a live voice on the other end. Swiping the screen, I went to the voicemail app and pressed the button for the message. With the phone to my ear, I listened to the woman's voice in lightly accented English.

I know what happened last night and think we can help each other. A text message will provide you an address where you will find your boat.

It sounded too good to be true. The screen buzzed again and I read the address, wondering how I was going to navigate the unmarked maze of desert roads and find it. I set the phone on the hand rest between the seats and glanced again at the address, this time realizing that it was a link. Pushing the highlighted text, the phone went dark and the maps app opened. It looked like it was searching for my position. A minute later, a message appeared in Spanish. I couldn't read it all, but two words did register: *no Internet.* With no choice, I started down the hill, figuring as long as I was losing altitude, I would at least find the umbrella of the Internet.

I descended, staying to roads that looked to go in the general direction of the city. The desert road followed a series of sharp switchbacks that would have been lined with guardrails in America. In several places I saw overturned trucks with vegetation growing over them on the side of the hill. As I descended, the landscape changed slightly, and I saw the man-made contours of a golf course.

With the first sign of civilization, I stopped to check the phone. Finally, my position was highlighted, and a route to the rendezvous showed in blue. The roads here were not marked, but as long as I stayed near the line, I would eventually find the woman and the *Nai'a.*

I knew I was being naive, dealing with murderers and gangsters. There was no way this woman was going to welcome me aboard and thank me for my service, but I would have to deal with that when I got there. I counseled myself to remember this sage advice and not say yes just because she had a nice smile. I decided to take a cautious approach.

The road turned from rutted gravel to a bumpy asphalt-like surface. Soon I was out of the hills and cruising on pavement. The phone spoke to me, giving directions to my destination, and I found myself driving through the town. Poverty encompassed the outskirts of the city, with shacks lining the road. Soon the ramshackle buildings were replaced by rectangular cinder block houses with rebar sticking out of their flat roofs, waiting to support a second story that would never be built. I soon found myself in a more commercial area, and the phone said my destination was on the right.

I could see no water from where I parked, not even the tips of masts indicating that *Nai'a* was close by. Whoever I was meeting was not going to just hand over the boat, but I really hadn't expected them to. The town square was off to the right, and the cafe with the address over the door was to the left. Thunder rumbled in the background, and I remembered the red hue to the sky this morning. Cautiously I entered, just as the first fat drops of rain started to fall.

The smell of coffee was strong coming from the burlap sacks stacked along the side wall. There was a small counter and a dozen or so tables, mostly taken. I stood there, trying not to look foolish, but wondering what to do. A voice took me by surprise, beckoning me to the counter. I approached, and the barista handed me a mug and motioned with her eyes to a table in the corner. A woman sat alone, reading a newspaper, the wide brim of her hat concealing her face.

As I approached, I couldn't help but notice the well-defined copper legs revealed by her slit skirt. My eyes followed her legs up her body, that though covered in the loose cloth of her dress, appeared to have all the right curves in all the right places. The brim of the hat moved as I set my mug down and pulled out the chair. The turquoise eyes that greeted me took my breath away. It was not an especially welcoming look, more as if she knew that I was evaluating her and didn't care for it.

"Sit down and stop staring," her lightly-accented voice said.

I sat, but found the staring part hard not to do. Now that I could see her face, I forgot about her body. Small freckles that converged on her nose accented her eyes, giving her an exotic and intriguing look. I moved the chair slightly so I was not looking right at her and sat. "Hello," came out of my mouth.

"You are Will Service?" she asked.

I just nodded. I wasn't sure how well I could put words together and tried to remember my mantra—don't say yes.

"Your boat is safe."

That was good news. "The message on the phone said that I could have her back," I said.

"Yes, we will keep our word, but--"

Thunder struck, a loud sharp boom, and in its aftermath I heard rain, fast and hard on the roof.

"But what?" I asked.

"This storm is going to be bad. We should go before the arroyo floods," she said, standing and moving toward the door.

I had no choice but to follow. She exited first and turned toward the street, asking me with her eyes where I had parked. I led her across the street to the car. The rain was hot, hard, and heavy, soaking us both by the time I opened the passenger door for her. I ran around the front and got in the driver's side. We sat there for a minute as another thunderclap vibrated through the interior.

"It will let up in a few minutes. The storms here are never long, but they will cause flooding and sometimes close the roads. We need to go."

I could barely see the front of the hood, but I got the urgency in her voice. I started the car and pulled out cautiously. She directed me out of town, and we were soon following Federal

Highway 1 south toward Cabo. I had questions, but the rain was too loud to talk over, and navigating the road ahead took all my concentration. We were soon out of town, and the sky lightened slightly, but another thunderclap brought me back to reality. The road was deserted, with a line of cars and trucks pulled off to the side, choosing to wait out the storm—obviously smarter than I was.

Fifteen minutes later, my knuckles started to hurt from my death grip on the wheel, but the storm was still raging. Ahead I could barely make out a torrent of water.

"Hurry," she yelled over the rain.

I saw what she was worried about now. A long bridge stood in front of me. I couldn't see its end, and it had a river running fast and hard underneath it. The powerful stream seemed to be rising and gaining strength with every raindrop. I gripped the wheel harder and pressed the gas pedal down. The Jeep picked up speed, and just as I thought we had made it, the first wave crossed the pavement, washing water over the road. I fought the wheel and slowed, trying to keep the hydroplaning tires on the pavement, but skidded into the guardrail.

"Keep your speed up," she screamed.

I followed her order and slammed my foot hard on the gas. The vehicle responded and started to straighten out, but the water was higher now, and the road almost invisible. All I could do was hold the wheel straight and hope for the best. Finally the bridge ended and we were on solid ground. As if on cue, the sky lightened ahead and the rain slowed.

"That bridge will be closed at least the rest of the day," she said.

I wasn't sure how this was important to recovering the *Nai'a*, so I just nodded. What I really wanted was another look at her, but I stared straight ahead. Soon the rain ended, and faint rays of sun emerged from the clouds. Steam came off the asphalt, and in a few more minutes the storm was gone.

Chapter 8

There was little evidence of the storm as we entered the marina district of Cabo San Lucas a half hour later. It looked like business as usual in any tourist town, with cafes and restaurants opening and a steady stream of boats leaving the harbor. She directed me to a parking spot a good quarter mile from the harbor.

"Why so far away?" I asked as we started walking down a side street.

"Better that they don't know we have the Jeep," she said.

"Are you going to tell me who *they* are and who *you* are?" She continued walking ahead of me. I lengthened my stride and caught her.

She turned to me. "It is a simple matter, really, you just walked in at the right time. I assure you our goals are in line."

"Really? I don't run around killing people," I said.

"I said our goals, not our means. You are in way over your head, thinking you can take down a man like Sam Chuy by yourself."

"I'm just after the boat. I don't have any interest in Chuy," I said.

"And you think it is that simple with the woman aboard?" she asked, pulling me into an alley, clearly frustrated by my persistence. "My brother told you what we are dealing with?"

I nodded. We were face–to–face now. "I can always walk

away," I said.

"With nothing, yes, you can. Go ahead. I will not stop you," she said, moving to the side.

I stood there trying to think my way through this puzzle, realizing that there was too much at stake to walk away. "So, if I help you, then what?"

She gave me a reassuring smile, which I wasn't sure was real. "You get both boats."

"Why me?"

"Let's just say you appeared conveniently. Let's just say it's in our best interest that the boat is taken legally and no one knows what has happened."

"And if this woman, your sister, you are looking for just happens to be aboard when I take it . . . ?"

"Then you will have made some powerful friends. Gerardo is more than just a soccer player here—he is a national figure with great influence. So, you see, this is a win–win for both of us," she said, touching my arm.

I thought about the word *influence* and how that could solve my passport problem. Then I calculated the bounty on both boats. I was rationalizing now, and I knew I had fallen into another one of those situations where I couldn't say no.

"Can you tell me about the woman?" I asked. If I was going to risk my life, I should at least know whom I was doing it for.

She looked down, but not before I saw a tear form in her eye. "My sister."

One side of my brain thought I was being played, but the other nodded and said, "We'll get her back."

Still unsure of what forces ruled my mind, we left the alley and started walking down to the marina. The storm had at least temporarily sucked the humidity from the air, and the afternoon sky was now a vibrant blue. The streets became more crowded as we approached the water.

I ignored the crowds, focusing instead on how I was going to take the boat. The tops of the sailboats' masts poked above the buildings as we approached the harbor. She stopped me and walked into a T-shirt store, coming out a few minutes later with a tacky trucker's hat, which she handed to me. She placed her hat on her head, adjusting the brim to conceal her face, and I followed her lead and lowered the bill on mine.

"Are you going to tell me where my boat is?"

"Just off the beach, where you left it," she said, as if it had been there the whole time.

The harbor was busy, with charter boats and water taxis moving in and out. I was worried about the *Nai'a* and her lack of adequate ground tackle. The storm had been strong enough to easily pull her light anchor and send her to sea or the beach. Whoever had outfitted her had obviously been more comfortable in marinas than anchoring. If it were me, not only would I have chosen a heavier anchor, but I would have increased the chain rode and added more and heavier line.

I led her back to the dock where I had left the dinghy, hoping it was still there. We passed the entrance to Chuy's dock, and we both lowered the brims of our hats as we passed. I could see the sportfisher out of the corner of my eye. There was activity on the deck—too much for a boat in port. Picking up the pace, we reached the dock where I had left the dinghy.

The inflatable was nowhere in sight. Whether torn loose by the storm, or taken, I had no idea. I only knew we were stranded. Just to make sure it hadn't been blown underneath by the storm, I went down on my belly and scanned the water underneath the structure. There was no sign of it.

"The dinghy's gone."

"We'll get another if you need it. As I said before, money is not a problem," she said.

I looked around the marina, not thinking that I would find a dinghy dealer nearby. Marcella was on her phone when I saw the superstructure of the *Dorado* start to move. It slid backward, and a moment later the bow emerged and turned into the main channel.

"They're leaving," I said.

She lifted her head from her phone, and we both watched the boat idle toward the back of the harbor. "But they're going farther into the harbor."

I watched the boat move away, scanning the decks to see how many were aboard. "Check for fuel docks. I bet that's what they're doing. No one moves a boat that size unless they have to."

She looked down again, and I watched her work the screen with her two thumbs. "You're right," she said, holding the phone out for me to see. There was a red dot directly ahead of Chuy's boat showing a fuel icon.

"We need to get back to the sailboat." I scanned the water for a way to the boat, but she had beaten me to it and flagged a water taxi. Marcella and the driver went back and forth in Spanish, spoken too quickly for me to comprehend, negotiating across the three-foot gap between the taxi and the dock. It appeared they reached an agreement, and the pilot skillfully maneuvered the boat to rest against the dock. She stepped down to the deck and I followed. Giving the man a command, she motioned him toward the inlet. He waited. Finally, she fished a small purse from a fold in her dress and handed him several bills.

The boat jerked forward, causing me to grab for the splintered wooden overhang. Marcella started to say something, but stopped in mid-sentence. The engine, running loud without a muffler, made it hard to talk.

I was more interested in prayer at the moment. The storm had been short, but intense, and I was worried about the *Nai'a*. We left the inlet, and, using hand signals, I instructed the driver to turn to port and follow the beach to the north. As we closed on the location I had anchored the morning before, I scanned the horizon for a sign of her. The mast should have at least been visible by now, and I realized that my fears had likely come to fruition. At this point, I could only hope that we could find her and she was salvageable.

I was down two boats and probably a job if I couldn't recover the *Nai'a*. Chuy fueling his boat left no doubt in my mind that he was moving on. Without the *Nai'a*, following him would be close to impossible. His sportfisher was four times faster than the best the *Nai'a* could do motor-sailing, but I wasn't worried as long as the radar transponder continued to broadcast his location. I was confident that once he reached his next destination, he would remain there for a while. He didn't seem like the cruising kind of guy. Hopping from small port to small port, having to run his air conditioning off a generator, and the lack of Internet were just a few inconveniences that cruisers dealt with. Some relished the nomadic lifestyle—the others kept me in business.

We were within a quarter mile of where I remembered anchoring, and there was no sign of the mast. With my hand shading my eyes to reduce the glare, I scanned the horizon for any sign of her. The driver startled me with a nudge and handed me a pair of binoculars. I adjusted them and turned first to seaward, making sure she was not adrift, hoping that this was the case. The horizon was empty, and I turned to the beach.

"There she is," I said, pointing to a rock-lined shore. I had anchored in the middle of a long stretch of beach, but the current running to the north acted like a magnet, sucking anything it could toward the rocks. "The mast is still intact," I said, studying the predicament. She had not yet reached the rocks, but she was close. My future was in the hands of the water taxi driver.

"*Vamanos*," I said, pointing to the shore.

"No, *señor*. It is too dangerous," he said, changing to broken English.

I turned to Marcella. "Pay him whatever he wants. We have

48

no time."

She grasped the urgency of the situation, and I couldn't help but admire her skill, using the perfect mix of pesos and smiles to negotiate with the driver. Whatever she did worked. He spun the wheel and accelerated, looking to my outstretched hand for our course. I struggled with the movement of the boat and the binoculars, abandoning the later once I could see the mast.

We came up on her fast, and the driver looked to me, clearly not knowing what to do. The extent of his boat training was probably shuttling tourists around the harbor and, when the seas permitted, taking them to Lovers Beach and the Arch. A quick look at *Nai'a* swinging wildly in the unsettled water created by the surge and subsequent backwash forced me to action.

"Have him find a line," I told Marcella, giving her instructions to tie it to the port cleat on the stern and coil the remainder. "We need about a hundred feet. Have him cut the anchor line if need be." I moved him from the helm and cut the wheel to take the taxi downwind of the *Nai'a*. The last thing I needed was to collide with her before we were ready. So far, Marcella had done as she promised, but having to reimburse someone for a totaled water taxi might not be in the program.

The driver had several dock lines laid out on the deck. "It's no good," I called out to Marcella. "They're shredded, and he can't tie a knot." His attempts at a sheet bend looked too similar to a granny knot for me to trust them. "We're only going to get one shot at this. Pull the anchor line out."

Chapter 9

I looked at the anchor line strewn on the deck. It was in better shape than the dock lines. I would have preferred something thicker. Actually, I would have preferred a lot of things, but I had what I had. The man pulled a knife from his pocket and, at Marcella's urging, was about to cut the line at the chain when I had an idea.

"No," I yelled. "Leave it."

The man looked confused.

"What do you want?" Marcella sounded frustrated.

Her tone made me feel incompetent, which I may be, but with the *Nai'a* about to hit the rocks, I was out of time. "Have him bring the taxi as close as he can. I'm going to throw the anchor and hope it grabs something," I said, waiting for her to translate.

The driver took the wheel and I went for the anchor. Glancing up several times as I readied the line, I could see he understood what I wanted. The gap between the boats was now only a hundred feet. I guessed the length of anchor line at about the same, and waited. I knew I was out of time when I heard the unmistakable sound of fiberglass scraping against rock. I breathed deeply, knowing I had to be patient. With the anchor and a dozen coils in my right hand, I moved to the gunwale and waited for the next swell to crest. At the high point of the wave, I threw the anchor with everything I had. The coils released evenly, and I jumped back to let the momentum take the rest of the line that was coiled on the deck.

I cringed at the sound of fiberglass tearing again. I wasn't sure if it was the anchor or the boat hitting the rocks and didn't care. Tapping the driver on the shoulder, I pointed out to sea. Waves crashed over the stern, flooding the deck as he put the engine in reverse. Slightly relieved, I watched the anchor line pay out. We were at least moving away from the rocks. I had to wonder what Marcella had promised him to risk both his life and his boat. Backing into seas this size was a dangerous task, but we didn't have time to move the anchor line to the stern, which would allow us to tow the sailboat properly. I hadn't checked if the bitter end was secured to the boat and could only hope it was sufficiently tied off in the compartment. Attempting to tie off the line to a cleat now could take my hand off. He slowed as the line pulled out of the water, violently shaking water from its fibers, and a second later the boat seemed to stop.

The spray from a wave hitting one of the rocks cascaded over the deck, soaking us, and I thought I had miscalculated and was about to send two boats to the depths. A wave smashed into the transom and time seemed to freeze. I felt us move slightly. Instead of just raising the boat like we were anchored, the resistance told me we were moving. Seconds later, Marcella and the driver smiled, realizing we had made it. Another wave crashed over us, and the smiles changed to determined looks. The water was ankle deep in the hull. I looked around, but the deck was below the waterline, making self-bailers impossible. I could only hope he had a working bilge pump, but, even with that, at the volume the waves were dumping water into the boat, it would never keep up.

We were away from the grasp of the rocks now. "Get him to turn the taxi into the waves. I'm going to board the boat."

"You're what?"

"There's no choice. We're taking on too much water like this," I said. She did as I asked, and the driver turned the bow into the waves. The anchor line was my worry now as it stretched across the old wooden hull. Not really sure of the consequences, but knowing there was no other way to save the boat, I grabbed the line and lowered myself into the water. At least now, if the line broke, I was connected to the *Nai'a*. Not a very good connection, but there nevertheless.

Hand over hand, I worked closer to the sailboat, but the forward motion was dragging me under. I gave Marcella a thumbs-down signal, hoping she would know what I wanted. She turned to the driver and the boat slowed. I could move now and continued pulling myself along the line to the sailboat. Exhausted, I pulled to within twenty feet of the bow rail, but where the line left the water to cross over the rails, I slipped and lost my grip. The boats were dead in the water, but the current was running strong enough to pull me back toward the stern of the sailboat. About to lose it, I kicked hard toward the transom, reaching out for the swim ladder.

The boats were falling back toward the rocks now, and there was nothing that Marcella or the driver could do to help me when something smashed against my leg. I felt the bottom rung of the ladder and grabbed. With everything I had left, I pulled myself toward the sailboat. I had two hands on the ladder and relaxed slightly, and, with a deep breath, pulled myself out of the water and aboard the boat. Marcella must have seen me gain the deck and let out a hoot that took me by surprise. I wanted to yell back, but the ground we had lost drifting backward had brought us within striking distance of the rocks again.

Making my way to the helm, I started the engine. My work on the trip up paid off and it started immediately and, as if sensing the dire straits the boat was in, reacted eagerly to my touch when I engaged the transmission and pushed the throttle forward. Her bow sliced through the water, but now I risked fouling the propeller with the towline. Adding ten degrees to the autopilot, I watched the bow swing toward open water, and, using the shrouds for support, I gained the foredeck and crawled to the water taxi's anchor.

The hatch over the main stateroom had saved the boat but suffered the consequences. Its plastic cover was broken, allowing the anchor to grab the deck. Standing, I signaled Marcella to have the driver reverse the taxi and waited for enough slack to come out of the line to release its hold on the boat. As soon as I could, I pulled the flukes from the opening and tossed the anchor over the side. The boat was free now, and I made my way back to the helm and released the autopilot.

I breathed deeply, knowing the worst was over and the boat and I had made it through, adding another bond to the growing list of trials we had endured together. I stood off from the taxi, allowing the driver to retrieve his anchor before sidling up to his gunwale.

Marcella pulled her purse out and handed the driver a wad of pesos. He took them and stuffed them in his pocket, then showed his experience gained in maneuvering in the tight quarters of the harbor. The driver worked the throttles and wheel of the taxi, calmly tossing a pair of fenders over the port rail just before the two boats touched. I reached a hand over to Marcella, who grabbed it and stepped across to board the *Nai'a*.

I set the autopilot again and went below. The storm had made my poor housekeeping look worse, and I scrambled to put things in order, but mainly I was checking for damage.

"I hope you have a plan, taking us this far out," she said, sticking her head in the companionway.

I ignored her, intent on finishing my survey. There were no apparent breaches in the hull, and the bilge was as dry as could be expected after what the boat had been through. The pump was running, removing what little water remained. Relieved, and slightly seasick from being below, I went to the deck and sat across from her in the cockpit. This was the first time since I had met her that we weren't rushing to or from a crisis, and I took my time to watch her before speaking.

Confidence with women was not one of my strengths, and although I would surely notice someone of her natural beauty, I would never have dreamed of being on a sailboat alone with her. And then it happened. All of a sudden, my mind shifted from danger mode to normal Will mode and I felt shy and insecure. Despite what we'd just been through, I was unsure what to say or do around her. Fortunately, she broke the tension I felt by pulling out her phone.

"What about Chuy?" she asked.

I had been daydreaming about other things, and it took me a minute to snap back to reality. "As long as his transponder is active you can look on Marinetraffic.com." She went back to her phone, manipulating the screen with her fingers and effortlessly typed in commands, while I resumed my daydream of being with her in ways that would never happen.

"There he is," she said, and handed me her phone.

The blue dot was moving in almost a direct line to the mainland. I knew if I could see movement on this small screen, they were running full out—probably forty-plus knots. I took control of the boat from the autopilot and changed course to the general direction he was heading.

"Know anything about sailing?" I asked.

"Not much," she said.

"From his course, we'll have a couple hundred miles of ocean to cross. Ready for your first lesson?" I asked her.

She nodded, and we got to work. Getting underway was always one of my favorite things about sailing. The moment when the sails took over from the motor and all you could hear were the waves against the hull and the wind in the rigging was something I always looked forward to. It was even better this time, watching her move around the deck, and I couldn't help but admire her agility and desire to learn. She looked like she was enjoying herself.

I showed her how to raise the mainsail and work the winches. With the jib out, we picked up speed, and I pointed out the telltales on the sails. When we had her trimmed right, I went to the helm and shut off the engine. I knew the look on her face and smiled to myself, happy to be in the company of a fellow sailor. We went through a quick tack and came about, so she would know what I needed her to do and what to expect from the boat, and then turned and jibed. The boom crashing over your head for the first time intimidated a lot of sailors, but it didn't seem to faze her.

"Can you take her?" I moved away from the wheel.

"What do I do?"

"Just keep us on ninety degrees." I tapped the compass. "Better to get on course and pick a cloud or landmark ahead," I said.

"Okay," she smiled.

I went below to retrieve my charts and sat across from her. It was hard to concentrate, and she caught me sneaking a look at her several times, but just smiled. For now, and the next twenty-four hours until we made landfall, the world would be at peace.

Chapter 10

For the next few hours we worked together, her learning the boat, and me trying to learn to be around her. It was not that I didn't appreciate the company or the scenery, but I was constantly aware of her. Used to doing most things solo, it was uncomfortable and awkward. By the time the sun had set, I was drained and had to figure out how to get through the night.

"Why don't you take the first watch," I offered. "I just need a couple of hours' rest, and I'll take it until dawn."

She gave me a scared look. "Do you think I'm ready for that?"

"Just point and shoot. The wind will drop, so you might have to adjust the sails. Otherwise just steer ninety degrees. Pick a star and follow it. If something changes, wake me," I said, going below to not give her any options. I had tried to check the position of Chuy's boat several minutes ago, but we had no reception. Until we reached the coast, we had no way to know where he was. I suspected Puerto Vallarta, the larger port. A place where a man with Chuy's tastes could get them satisfied. A seasoned cruiser might choose Mazatlan, a logical choice for the most direct crossing. I decided to stay with the most direct course. We could always follow the coast to Puerto Vallarta.

I was still too wired to sleep right away, so I made two sandwiches, brought them on deck, and handed one to Marcella.

"I thought you were trying to sleep," she said, taking the offering.

"Can't have the crew starving," I said, trying to discreetly check our course. She was doing fine, and the only thing I had to worry about was her falling asleep. "Why don't you set the alarm on your phone for ten and wake me then," I said, and went below. It was cooler now. The seas were down, and, at the eight knots we were traveling, the broken forward hatch funneled a nice breeze through the cabin.

Sailing was an odd thing. Time moved differently. There was a rhythm to it, a kind of primal feel, like this was the speed that life should move at. It would take us almost a full night and day to cover the same water that Chuy had probably already passed in a few hours, but it just felt right. I knew from experience that even though eight knots sounded ridiculously slow, the miles would add up.

Laying down on the forward V berth, I started putting together what I knew about Chuy, which was little. One thing I knew for sure: everyone suddenly seemed to die when they were about to tell me about him. That was not a good omen, and I thought about the woman above. She seemed benign, maybe playing the part on purpose. There was a cold, calculating part of her that I had admired at first, but now I thought I might have caught a glimpse of her true soul. This game they were playing was over my pay grade. Before I fell asleep, I concluded that Marcella was more competent than she had let on, and I had no worries about her standing a four-hour watch.

* * *

I was dreaming of the *Nai'a* anchored in gin-clear water off a perfect white sand beach when she shook me awake.

"Morning," Marcella said.

STEVEN BECKER

I jumped up wondering what had happened. It felt like I had been asleep longer than four hours.

"Morning?" I asked.

"It's just about two a.m.," she said. "I thought I'd let you sleep."

I shook my head, trying to untangle the cobwebs separating dreams from reality. "You didn't have to do that," I said, swinging my feet to the deck and stretching before I rose and slammed my head against the low bulkhead. "Thank you, though. I guess I needed it."

"*De nada,*" she replied. "My turn."

Without another look she rolled onto the berth and curled up. I watched her as she moved her hips to get comfortable and wanted to stay, but remembering the feeling I got when she caught me staring at her earlier, I took one last glance to hold me for the next four hours and headed up to the deck.

The brilliance of the night took my mind off her. There was a special feeling about being at sea on a clear night. The moon was a sliver, just the faintest hint of a crescent near the horizon, allowing the stars to show their full glory. This far from any light, the Milky Way was bright enough to look like a distant cloud. I picked the few stars I knew to use for navigation and went back to the helm.

She had done well. The autopilot had a hold of the boat, and the sails were trimmed to within a half turn of perfection. Not wanting to wake her, I left everything as it was and went to the chart plotter. The screen showed a small icon in the shape of a boat, facing east. The only thing surrounding us were hundreds of fathoms of water. I zoomed the screen out to show our position, about halfway between the Baja peninsula and the mainland—roughly eighty miles to go.

There was not much to do on a night watch in calm weather, so I trimmed the sails and went below for my backpack. In a gallon Ziploc bag was a spool of fishing line and several lures. When all else fails—fish. I unwound the line and tied a six-foot piece of the hundred-pound leader material I had to a fat swivel, and then tied on a bright pink lure. At night, the color wouldn't matter, but this one had a molded plastic concave head that would send a bubble stream behind it. If there were game fish around, they would hear it.

Carefully, I let out the line, one loop at a time. When it was all out, I pulled a bungee cord from the pouch and hooked one end to the loop tied a few feet from the end of the monofilament line. The other end went on the cleat along with the loop tied in the end of the fishing line. The bungee cord was pulled tight, allowing enough slack in the fishing line that when a fish hit, the elastic cord would take the brunt of a strike, both setting the hook and alerting me that a fish was on. This was much heavier gear than I would have used with a rod and reel, but without the leverage of the rod or the drag of the reel to assist, it was me against the fish. A large billfish would probably break off, but that was all right. I was looking for a tuna or a dorado.

The hours wore on with little to do but hope for a fish and think. The fish didn't come, but with the line out, at least if felt like I was doing something. My thoughts, though, spiraled around in my head, running the gamut from dropping Marcella in Puerto Vallarta and taking off for the States, to the inevitable affair we would have once I rescued her sister. Both extremes were out of the question. I had the feeling, although the threat was never made, that I was in this for the long haul. Neither side of the battle I had fallen into had any reservations about killing someone in their way. In that regard, Mexico was living up to its reputation.

The bounty on the *Dorado* was the deciding factor. I had become attached to the *Nai'a* and was thinking about making an offer to Salvage Solutions for her. I could easily live aboard the cruiser in San Diego. Then, with the money I would get from Chuy's boat, I would jet down to the tropics once or twice a year, bail out a distressed cruiser and sail the boat back for a nice profit. But the obstacles standing in the way of my dream all had guns and weren't afraid to use them.

An idea came to me just as the first hint of day highlighted the predawn sky. It was just about to form when I heard a loud snap that jerked me to attention.

Something splashed a few hundred feet behind the boat, and I ran for the hand line. Fighting a fish by hand was much different than by rod and reel. It was strength against strength, and the only way the fish was going to win was if the line broke or the hook pulled. The momentum of the boat would hurt in the beginning, but would eventually assist me in the fight by drowning the fish. It wasn't very sporting, but I was after a fresh meal, not a fight.

Hand over hand, I pulled the fish toward the transom. After anticipating a few jumps, I knew I had a nice dorado on. Tuna would sound, but dorados stayed on the surface. It was just a matter of hanging on until the boat did the work, but then I would have a problem. Tying the line around a cleat, I scanned the cockpit for anything I could use as a gaff or, at the very least, a club to knock the fish out before I brought it aboard. Dorados were hard fighters in the water, but once on a deck they reached a frenzy, slamming their bodies against anything within striking range. I had several scars on my shins to attest to their sharp fins and unquenchable spirit.

The only thing not tied down was the winch handle. I grabbed it from its holder and set it by the transom door. With the line back in my hands, I pulled sharply, checking to see how green the fish was. It gave a quick tug as if it wanted to make a run, but it was short-lived, and I knew the heavy line was taking a toll on it. The risk now was the hook pulling from its mouth as the entry point enlarged and softened from the fight. A single jerk could set it free.

As I pulled it closer to the stern, I thought I saw a fin

swimming behind it, but there was nothing I could do. If it was a shark, it would take part of the fish, if it was another dorado, I had no interest. One was enough. I pulled harder in case it was the former, and the dark green head appeared on the surface. Reaching for the winch handle, I opened the transom door and braced myself against the opening. Another two pulls and the fish was within reach. With a single overhand shot, I landed a blow to the head that took the fight from him. A few more pulls and he was lying in the cockpit.

"What are you doing?" Marcella stood in the companionway, rubbing sleep from her eyes.

I stepped aside proudly, showing the twenty-pound fish to her. "Breakfast?"

"*Si*, and then we have a problem," she said, handing me the phone.

Chapter 11

"The woman is awake," the thick-chested man said to Chuy.

"Bring her up," he said, without looking up from his computer.

The connection was slow but secure. His tech guy had assured him of that. He scrolled down the news page, checking both ESPN and the other major sports websites. There was nothing about the girl. That was good. It meant the famous Gerardo had listened. Now all the star player for Mexico's national soccer team had to do was ensure a loss. The betting line heavily favored Mexico in the World Cup qualifier. As long as the star wanted his girlfriend back, he would cooperate. Chuy started to count the money he expected to make betting against the favorite, hoping it was enough to free him from exile.

His calculations were interrupted by the protest of the girl as she was dragged on deck. "Can you be a little nicer to our guest?" he scolded Frank, thinking there was no reason for him to be the bad guy as long as his muscle was around. *Hell, she might even come around and give me a little of that*, he thought, looking appreciatively at her body.

"Just one more day, sweetheart," he said.

She looked up, not understanding.

"*Mañana*, baby," he clarified and saw the anger in her eyes.

Frank must have seen it too. "You think we ought to give her another shot to calm her down some?"

"That would depend," Chuy said, moving toward the girl, now curled up on the deck. He reached down and petted her hair like she was a cat. "Maybe not just yet," he answered. There were two reasons he wanted her sober. The realistic one was that he didn't trust Frank with her; the delusional one was that she might want him.

He went back to the table and reached for the flip phone sitting next to his iPhone. Opening it, he went to the recent calls screen and hit the only number shown. Chuy checked the line on his laptop one more time in the long minute it took for the international call to go through. The odds were almost four-to-one now, and he added another twenty grand to his bet. That made a total of a hundred thousand of the quarter million he had planned. It was hard, but he knew he needed to be patient and dribble the bets slowly, or the line could be adversely affected.

Finally the call went through. A voice came on the other end.

"Is she well?" the accented voice asked.

Chuy handed the phone to the girl. She snatched it from his hand and immediately went into a tirade in Spanish. He thought about taking it back. If she was that much of a bitch in a situation like this, he could only imagine what she was like at home. Surprisingly, her feistiness made her more attractive to him, and he had to hide the growing bulge in his pants with the laptop. Finally, the rant ended and she said what seemed like some soothing words.

"Enough. If that was my woman blasting me like that, I'd leave her here to rot," he said to Frank, who took the phone from her. Chuy wiped the spittle from the phone before holding it to his head. "You see, she is fine."

"I have done as you asked. No authorities. No one knows, but you will release her after the game."

"Hell, I don't want her," Chuy said. "Just make it happen." He closed the lid on the phone, ending the call. The look on her face told him there was no chance at her making nice to him, and he instinctively backed away as if he were facing a poisonous snake. "Take her back down. Maybe give her that shot after all," he ordered Frank. He could have her then if he wanted.

He breathed deeply and sipped the lukewarm coffee, immediately spitting it over the side as the bitter taste hit his tongue. His forced exile to the third-world armpit was gnawing at him, and this plan was his last shot at getting back where he belonged. It was as simple as bringing a cool million back and handing it to his father. In fact, he planned on paying off his own bounty. See how the old man liked that. But placing his future on the foot of a Mexican soccer star and his hot but feisty girlfriend was unsettling. But, if this didn't work, he was doomed to crappy coffee and worse.

Frank interrupted his thoughts. "She's good now. Ought to sleep for most of the day if you want a shot at her."

"I prefer them live, but if that boyfriend of hers doesn't cooperate, she's all yours," he said, not failing to notice the look on Frank's face and wondering if he was actually on his side or if the lure of the girl or the bounty had compromised him. Something else to keep an eye on, he thought.

He was getting anxious and took several large deep breaths. It was distressing that he hadn't heard from his men back in Cabo, and he again cursed the third-world cell networks. There were too many areas with no or with sketchy coverage. Last night, one of his sources had reported that one of Gerardo's bodyguards had been seen ashore with the guy he had caught spying on him. If they hadn't been in the harbor, he would have blown the guy's head off, but that was not the right time or place. Instead of plugging him, he had restrained himself and ordered his men to follow them with direct orders to take them out. With no word from his men, he had to assume the worst and had fled the peninsula for the Mexican mainland.

Turning to shore, he stared over at the beach and dreamed of the half-naked women sunning themselves and playing in the water. The girls Frank had brought aboard in Cabo had been fun, but they were gone, dropped at the fuel dock before they left port. If the choice were his, he would have stayed on the Baja side, but he had felt the heat. Taking the girl there while her soccer star boyfriend and she were enjoying a few days at his ranch was part of the plan, but he had underestimated her family.

"Get the captain," he called to Frank. If he was stuck in this place, he at least needed a port where he could have some fun. Mazatlan had a harbor, but it was small. The resort town had insulated itself from the violence surrounding it by setting up its Golden Zone, where all-inclusive resorts kept their visitors behind gates, guarded by armed men to make them feel safe. There was a marina there, but it was too small and he would be noticed. What he needed was a more anonymous port where he could also satisfy his needs.

"Mr. Chuy," the man addressed him.

"*Hola*, Roberto. I'm hoping you are rested, because I want to move on," he said.

"Of course. We have fuel for another four hundred miles," the captain said.

He was not one of the inner circle, but Chuy got a good feeling from the man, and having a Mexican captain aboard had paid dividends several times already. Sending him the leftovers from his parties had probably helped as well. "I'm looking for something a little more interesting. Someplace we can blend in, that has a little more local flavor," Chuy said, winking at him.

The man smiled. It had been worth paying more for his English.

"Any ideas?"

Chuy looked down at the map he had opened on the laptop. "What about Puerto Vallarta?" He had noticed the large protected bay and large city.

"*Si*. Puerto Vallarta would be a good choice. The city is much bigger than Mazatlan and more diverse. The harbor is big enough that we would not attract any attention," he said.

Chuy looked up from his computer and smiled. The man had

been a good pick. He would be rewarded. He looked down dismissively, but the man remained in front of him. "Is there something else?"

"Two things, *jefe*," he said.

Chuy liked the *jefe* thing. "Go on."

"We should fuel before we leave," he said.

"I thought you said we had enough fuel for four hundred miles," he said, quickly Googling the distance from Mazatlan to Puerto Vallarta. "Are we talking miles or kilometers?" The web site said four hundred thirty-three kilometers, which was less than three hundred miles.

"Sorry, *jefe*. I mean miles. Under normal circumstances we could make it easily, but to be safe . . ."

"I'll worry about being safe. You just drive the boat," Chuy said. The man was starting to irritate him now.

"Very well, but there is one other thing you should know," he said.

Chuy didn't look up. "Yes."

"Maybe you would see this information as worthy of a bonus, *jefe*," he started.

If Chuy had a gun he would have shot him. The nerve of some third-world peon to ask for more money for doing his job. Breathing deeply, he put on the stone face he used with his enemies. "Yes."

"There is a radar transponder aboard that will tell anyone that is looking for you where we are."

Chuy relaxed his face. The captain was smarter than he thought. Maybe he did deserve a bonus. "You know how to disable this device?" he asked.

"*Si, jefe*, but it might be more useful to place it aboard another boat, maybe heading in the opposite direction," Roberto said, revealing two golden teeth when he smiled.

"You have done well, my friend. Yes, we will go into the harbor for fuel and follow your plan."

Chapter 12

"It's gone," Marcella said.

I took the phone and scanned the screen. The icon marking Chuy's boat was gone. "I was wondering when they would figure that out," I said, trying to hide my concern. The transponder and Chuy's desire to stop and party were the only things allowing us to keep pace with the cruising speed of the sportfisher.

"Can you keep watch for a few," I asked her, climbing backward down the three steps from the deck to the cabin. I took my laminated chart and a calculator to the table and started working some numbers. The boat probably carried a little over a thousand gallons of fuel and burned around eighty gallons an hour at a moderate cruising speed. The engines had a high end of forty knots and would burn considerably more fuel at that speed, but it would be an uncomfortable ride in these seas. Doing the math, I came up with a range of about four hundred miles. After the trip across the Sea of Cortez, she would have a little over five hundred gallons. I placed a dot on Mazatlan and, using the dividers, scribed a circle with a four-hundred-mile radius. With a full tank, he could cover a lot of ground.

I took the chart back on deck and sat across from Marcella, almost forgetting my reason for being there. Her skirt was hiked to mid thigh, showing a good mile of toned copper skin. "They'll be going for the harbor," I said, staring hard at the horizon ahead.

"How do you know that?" she asked.

I leaned over and showed her the chart. She leaned forward, showing me curves that I was not sure I was supposed to see. "The circle is his range on a full tank of fuel. He'd have about half that left when he made the coast," I said. "There's nowhere worth going to the north, and I don't think he'd want to be bottled up in the Sea of Cortez. Puerto Vallarta is my guess."

"That's another full day's sail. We need to do something now," she said, looking at the map.

We knew where he was now, and though we were only twenty miles away, it was a long two and a half hours. Put that way, a sailboat is a very slow form of transportation. "We'll need a plan, but first let's make sure he's here."

"Couldn't he have filled up and be on his way already?" she asked.

Possibly, but the fuel dock wouldn't have been open until this morning, and even if he was first in line, it takes time to fill a boat that size. But, she was right. He could have slipped our net already. I cut the wheel to starboard and set the autopilot on a hundred twenty degrees. The point of sail changed with the correction, and it took a few minutes to take the luff out of the sails before I could explain.

"We'll take the quickest route to land and follow the coast up to the harbor. That way if he left already we have a better chance of seeing him," I said, checking the telltales and making a few minor adjustments to the rigging.

I was on the foredeck, my hand to my brow to cut the morning glare. The *Nai'a* was moving well, and I climbed the first few rungs on the mast to gain some height, but also to distance myself from Marcella. I needed some time to come up with a plan without her questions.

A thin sliver on the horizon swiftly grew into low hills hiding the shadows of larger mountains behind them. Still without a plan, I watched the shore grow, keeping an eye out for the sportfisher.

"It's the land," I heard her say from the cockpit.

"We need to keep a close watch for Chuy now. If he's already fueled and underway, he should be just about here," I said, climbing down from my perch. I went back to the cockpit to adjust our course slightly to the north, trying to anticipate how far from shore Chuy would run. If it were me, I wouldn't follow the coast, but run a rhumb line straight to the northern point of the Bay of Banderas. That would put him within a mile east or west of our location.

"What about a plan?" she asked.

That was still a bit of a problem.

* * *

"Is this thing full yet?" Chuy called down to the deck. Roberto was straddling the gunwale with the gas hose between his legs and a towel ready for any overflow.

"*Cuanto ceasta?*" he called to the boy by the gas pump.

"*Dos cientos y veinte,*" the boy called back.

"Almost," he called up, "must have been some current on the crossing. We're over two hundred gallons."

Chuy did the math in his head. Another grand into the freakin' sea. This cruising thing was no fun at all. "They got any *puta* in this town?"

Roberto gave him a look as if to silence him. The boy working the pumps came and stood by the edge of the dock.

"I know some party girls," he said.

Chuy smiled, hoping they were the same age as he.

"Bring 'em by, boy. You deliver some primo goods, and I'll cut you in on the fun," he said and climbed down to the main deck. Gas spewed from the overflow valve just as he hit the bottom rung, but before he could scold him, Roberto had the towel ready and had cleaned the greasy residue off the fiberglass. He was becoming valuable too; maybe he'd get some leftovers.

"Once this pig's fueled up, put her in a slip. There's a game I want to catch," he said, sliding the door to the salon open. The cool air greeted him, almost freezing the sweat on his chest. Grabbing a Pacifico from the bar, he took the remote and started scanning the half dozen channels available without cable, cursing that there was only soccer.

"Frank. What the hell, man, can you get the USC game on that streaming thing you do? I got some money going down," he called out loud enough that anyone on board could hear him.

Frank came in with a laptop. "Could you hold it down a few decibels. I finally got enough in her to get her to sleep," he said.

"Shit." Between thinking about the young girls the boy had promised and topping off the bet on the soccer match, he had almost forgotten her. "Just got her to sleep, right." He stared at the screen, waiting for the game to appear. "Can you get this thing going, or what?"

"Just a minute. It's Mexico, you need to get a handle on things," Frank said, taking the laptop.

His attention was momentarily diverted when a grainy image appeared of both teams clumped together. USC was on the one yard line. He sat forward. The quarterback took the snap and stepped back. He extended his hand to the running back and the screen froze. "Mexico! I'm outta here as soon as the game is over tomorrow. Back to L.A., pay off the bounty, and back to civilization. Whatever happens, we're watching Lover Boy on a real TV."

"If things were always so easy," Frank muttered.

Chuy didn't hear him over the roar of the crowd as the team in white stopped the running back from scoring. He took a long pull on the beer, thinking he might need something more potent.

Ten grand was at stake on the game, not a lot under normal circumstances, but these days, having to worry about a stupid fuel bill, were what some called "interesting times."

The Trojans broke the huddle for third down, and he leaned forward again, clenching his hands, wondering if right over left was better luck than left over right. Tonight's party depended on this play. The screen started to pixilate, and he was about to lose it, but even with the poor signal he could see the quarterback take the snap, fake to the running back and slide through a hole between the guard and tackle. "Touchdown," he screamed, rising from the couch and raising his hands over his head. At least something was starting to go right.

Just then, the boat lurched as it moved away from the fuel dock. Chuy fell backward onto the couch and missed the penalty flag dropped behind the line of scrimmage. Seconds later, the boat spun and reversed again into the slip, but he didn't notice. He was back on his feet, screaming at the TV, watching the referee walk the ball back ten yards for holding. The next thing he knew, the field goal unit was marching onto the field, and he yelled again at the coach for having no balls.

The kick went through the uprights as the clock ticked down to zero, ending the game. USC won, but there was no joy in it for Chuy. The difference between the touchdown and the field goal had cost him the bet. Fortunately, he had hedged, not trusting his alma mater, and bet the under, making enough to pay for the fuel bill and party he had planned for later.

Frank and Roberto were securing lines to the stern cleats when he stepped out onto the deck. "Where'd the boy go?"

They both looked at each other.

"Tell the kid I only want one," he said and went back inside. "Screw those guys, screw the coach, screw 'em all," he said under his breath. He grabbed another beer from the refrigerator and popped the top, but before he drank any, he grabbed the bottle of tequila from the shelf and took a healthy swig. With the beer, he went back to the couch and spun around the laptop.

Navigating quickly between several sites, he checked the latest line on the soccer game and increased his wagers across the board. It was still holding at two goals and the same four-to-one payoff. Surely, with the girl below, this was easy money. Just as he was about to take a sip from the beer, the engines started and the boat jumped backward, again spilling beer on him. With a roar, he gained his feet, and bracing against the bulkheads, made his way to the door. He slid it open and saw the boat moving quickly backward. Wondering what was going on, he fell forward as the transmission was jammed into forward, kicking up a wake large enough to throw the adjacent boats into their pilings.

The stern swung to the dock as Roberto maneuvered out of the slip and into the channel.

A megaphone, held by a uniformed policeman, called, "*Alta.*" Standing beside the officer was the boy, with a smug look on his face. "Screw this two-bit town," he screamed over the roar of the engines. The crowd on the dock couldn't hear him, so he flipped them off and climbed the ladder to the bridge. First the USC coach and now this kid.

Chapter 13

"That's him," Marcella called from the foredeck.

I stood on my tiptoes for the best vantage point without leaving the helm. The towers of several sportfishers reflected the sunlight, but I couldn't tell if one was the *Dorado's* or not. The channel was my first concern. Entering a harbor for the first time, and without the benefit of a local cruising guide, took all my attention. The angle of the sun made it hard to see the color of the water, so I had to rely on my electronics. I watched the chart plotter and depth finder simultaneously, but neither would give me enough warning if I wandered into trouble. A single storm could shoal an inlet, making it impassable at low tide, and I had to hope that the channel was as deep as the markings on the chart indicated.

Mazatlan had two harbors; the larger and more commercial one was to the south, the northern one was what I figured to be more to Chuy's liking. As a precaution we had checked the larger harbor first, dropping sail in front of the entrance and just getting out of the way of the Mazatlan–La Paz ferry. There were several branches off the main channel, but this was not the kind of place Chuy would hang out. Under motor, we left the harbor and cruised north past two seamounts common to the coast here, staying to seaward of both. After passing the Island de Pejados, I saw the small inlet and turned toward the coast.

The smaller harbor was not as well marked on the charts, and I hoped a sailboat or motor cruiser would show me the way. Several small pangas cruised in and out of the harbor, but they could be misleading with their shallow draft and were no indication that the keel of the sailboat would pass. We came in dead center of the breakwaters on either side of the entry without incident, and I started to relax, knowing I was in the deep-water channel now.

Marcella stood with one hand on the mast and the other extended, pointing at something in the distance. The wind sculpted her skirt to her figure, and I was hard-pressed to follow her signal. The marina opened up ahead, but on the right were three finger piers with a mix of sailboats and cruisers. This was more like Chuy's neighborhood; large well-appointed sailboats and several sportfishers similar to his were docked here. She pointed emphatically, and I saw the *Dorado* ahead, backed into the last slip in the line.

Her position was well planned, making me wonder what kind of ruse I would need to get them off the boat. The slip was both a good observation post, with a clear view from the flybridge of anyone entering or leaving the harbor, and well positioned, with the bow facing forward for a quick escape. After dropping her dock lines, it was a straight shot to blue water. She could disappear in minutes.

They had either gotten lucky with the slip, or someone aboard had some tactical knowledge. I would have to assume the later and reviewed my two plans. Neither was well thought out, and one required taking the boat by force, something I was not equipped or trained for. Repossessing the boat would require me to figure out a way to get them off it. I couldn't see them all going ashore for a party. With the woman held below and the bounty on his head, I doubted Chuy would leave the boat in a strange port. I would have to come up with a way to get them all off. I figured I'd

74

need about ten minutes with Marcella's help to take her.

I also couldn't take the chance of Chuy noticing the *Nai'a*, Marcella, or me. He had clearly seen me and might remember the boat from Cabo. *Nai'a* had unique lines and a thick blue band painted on her white hull, making her memorable to anyone with an eye for boats. Marcella had told me she and Marisa, her sister, were often mistaken for twins, making her easy to spot, and I ordered her below. Then I pushed the throttle to the five-knot speed limit and ducked behind the helm as the *Nai'a* slid by the *Dorado*.

Risking a glance at her as we passed, I saw all the attention focused on a group of people standing on the dock. Several were uniformed, and even over the engine noise I could hear them yelling back and forth. Suddenly there was a loud roar and a cloud of smoke came from the *Dorado's* transom.

"What are they doing?" Marcella stuck her head out of the companionway.

"Something's going on. There are police on the dock, and he just started his engines." I had just seen a blast of black smoke come from his exhaust. She came beside me, and we watched two men go for the lines securing the transom of the boat to the dock, and with a loud roar she moved out of the slip. Their position allowed the quick escape I had worried about, and, leaving the men still yelling on the dock, the bow lifted and the propellers dug her stern into the water, putting up a large wake. Seconds later, the hull planed out and the boat cruised out of the harbor and disappeared. The remnants of the wake, looking like the contrail from a jet, were the only indication of where they were headed.

There was no need for subterfuge now, and I cut the wheel hard to port and pushed down the throttle to the limit. I followed the fading wake out of the harbor. There was no sign of the boat now, but the faint trail of foam showed her path to the south. I thought about putting up the sails, but the trade-off in time for three or four additional knots of speed wasn't worth it. I thought it better to follow as long as I had a trail, but it quickly dissipated, leaving me without any other indication than their general direction.

I looked around for Marcella, surprised she wasn't either forward searching for the boat that held her sister, or in the cockpit questioning me. I saw a glimpse of her below, and peering around the companionway saw her head down and thumbs working the screen of the phone.

"I thought we lost their signal," I called down to her.

I must have startled her, because she looked up like a fish seeing a gaff for the first time. "Just trying," she said, continuing to type on the small keyboard. "They must have fueled up and are heading for Puerto Vallarta."

My question went unanswered, and I again suspected that there was more to this than just getting her sister back. Like a child caught with her hand in the cookie jar, she stashed the phone in a compartment by the table and sauntered toward me. I had the wherewithal this time to file her activity in my memory before she came beside me and I forgot everything but her.

"We should take advantage of the wind before the sun sets," I said clumsily.

"You're the captain." She patted my arm, sending shivers like an electric shock through me. Then she went forward, and, like a good student, showed off what I had taught her.

The wind was behind us blowing from the northwest, putting the *Nai'a* on a beam reach, one of her best points of sail. She eagerly climbed the windblown rollers and picked up speed as she surfed down their faces. Marcella was beside me again.

"How long until we make Puerto Vallarta?" she asked.

"It'll be this time tomorrow, maybe later if the wind dies overnight," I said. The second seamount was to port, and we were just about to pass the commercial harbor. "If we run the engine we can maybe knock off a couple of hours."

"Will we have enough fuel?"

I did some quick calculations. "We'll need to refuel there if he makes another move."

"We should save some just in case," she said, pressing her body against mine. "And it's so much nicer without the noise. It makes me feel free."

The *Nai'a* seemed to sense the change and picked up another knot on her own when I shut off the engine. I felt Marcella's hand on my arm and glanced over at her, thinking she was doing it subconsciously. She certainly seemed to have taken to sailing. "We should split the watch again," I said.

"I don't like these schedules," she said and stuck her tongue in my ear.

Before I could question her motivations, I responded and pulled her to me. It had been a long time since I had been with a woman, and I let myself go. Giving control of the boat to the autopilot, I took her below.

It was faster than I would have liked, and the heat of the cabin pulled us apart. "I should check our position," I said, sliding off the berth. She lay there entangled in the sheets.

"Give me a few minutes and I'll make some food," she said and yawned.

"Take a nap if you want," I said, pulling on my shorts. "I'll take watch for a few hours."

"Sure. Wake me up when you're ready." She rolled onto her belly, showing me the fine curves of her back.

I grabbed my T-shirt, filled my water bottle from a gallon jug I had stuck in the small refrigerator, and went on deck. It was dark now, and fortunately the wind was still holding. I scanned the horizon for any signs of navigation lights and seeing none looked down at the chart plotter. We were running parallel with the coast. After adjusting the autopilot for a course that would hold us about five miles offshore to avoid any local traffic, I went below for my charts.

Her cell phone was beside them in the same compartment. Curious, I picked it up. Just as I did, the screen flashed with a message. I glanced at Marcella sleeping on her side and took the phone above.

I knew I had acted out of total lust and scolded myself for not showing some restraint. Her behavior had been suspicious since we left port. I stared at the message, but only understood a few words of the Spanish text.

Chapter 14

Chuy finally relaxed when Roberto came down from the bridge to tell him they had crossed into Jalisco. He wasn't really sure about Mexican geography or the power each state had, but now that they were two provinces removed from Mazatlan and the authorities there, he felt more comfortable. He looked out the window and saw, just visible in the distance, the point hiding the entrance to the Bay of Banderas. It was still a dozen miles off, but he could feel the party atmosphere of the port already.

After the game tomorrow night, he would enjoy the town, but for now, he had learned a valuable lesson—these people were not to be trusted. He would remain aboard until the match was over and his winnings were wired into his bank account. Internet service had been sporadic on the way down, and he had seen the line fluctuate several times. It took a lot more discipline than he was used to, but dribbling the bets in had worked. He now had over a quarter of a million dollars on the game—a potential million-dollar payoff.

Tomorrow morning he would call Gerardo and let him speak to his girlfriend again, just to reassure him what was at stake. He had thought about calling L.A. and brokering the deal with his father to pay off the bounty on his head, but decided against it. Before he made that call, the money needed to be in the bank. And as he had seen, things happened down here—and not always in his favor.

He sat on the deck in a padded fishing chair, his shirt open to the breeze. It was hot, but the heat was mitigated by their cruising speed, and the cold beer in his hand didn't hurt either. It had been a long couple of days, running around the ocean, burning money for fuel. He'd originally bought the boat as a chick magnet, to sit in port and party. Now, since he had been on the run, it had proved useful.

Half an hour later, they rounded the point, and the view of the city climbing up the hills lifted his spirits. Starting on the beach, he watched the high-rise hotels and condominiums grow smaller and blend into more modest buildings. The red tile roofs accented the green landscape, a stark change from the dessert he'd been looking at for days. Further up the hill he could see areas of spectacular homes with panoramic views of the Pacific, but it was the smaller neighborhoods of lower-class workers that made him smile. It was these pockets of poverty that provided the women and girls he favored. Those that would do anything for a few pesos. The diverse mix of the city was the first real sign of his kind of civilization he had seen since leaving the States.

"*Señor*, there are several marinas here, do you have a preference?" Roberto called down from the flybridge.

Climbing the ladder to the bridge, he stood next to Roberto at the helm and pointed at the tallest building on the beach. "There."

* * *

I had been at the helm since midnight. Marcella had risen around six and cooked some of the fish I had caught, then allowed me a nap. The winds had been favorable through the night, and, even without the added knots the motor would have given us, we were ahead of schedule. To conserve battery power, I had shut down the electronics and all power except the navigation lights and steered by the stars. Without the distraction of the glare from the screens, I could see for miles. It had been an easy run with a following sea, giving me time to plan my next move. It was vague and complicated by the two women, especially the one sleeping below. I had succumbed to her charm, though, at the same time, I was wary that something wasn't right.

Once I was sure she was asleep, I had checked her phone again, but our course had taken us too far offshore to get a signal. The messages and emails were all in Spanish, beyond my dozen-word vocabulary. The lack of reception foiled my plan to use Google translate to decipher the text.

The long night had given me time to think—too much time. I was still thinking about dumping Marcella in Puerto Vallarta, forgetting about Chuy, and heading back to San Diego with the *Nai'a*. That was the easy way, and I knew deep down that if I wanted to break the mold and do something for myself, that I needed to see this through—the reward would be my freedom. I also had to admit that I was more than intrigued by the woman sleeping below.

As the first tendrils of sunlight filtered through clouds, she appeared in the companionway. It all seemed so perfect that my suspicions vanished along with the darkness. In the light of day, everything looked better.

"Where are we?" she asked.

"Morning. Turn on the batteries and I'll power up the electronics," I said.

I stared after her, watching the sway of her hips as she climbed down the steps to the cabin. A few seconds later the beeping of the electronics brought my focus back. The chart plotter cycled through its startup screens, and once it acquired a signal, showed the boat as an icon overlaid on a chart. "About three quarters of the way out in the middle of nowhere," I answered. We were at our furthest position from land on the rhumb line I had plotted, the most direct path possible, with a slight deviation to take the wind and seas into account. "Nothing to do for a while. Want to take the wheel, and I'll cook some breakfast?"

"Sure." She brushed against me, holding our bodies together for a moment before taking the wheel. "Same course?"

"For another hour or so, then we'll check and correct for the wind and current. Steer the compass; I'm going to shut off the batteries." I stood in the galley, chopping some onions, garlic, and celery to sauté with the fish. The course I had plotted had us on a nice beam reach with the gentle rollers coming from the starboard aft quarter, making for a smooth ride. One eye was on the knife; the other kept wandering to sneak a glance at her. After chopping the veggies, I released the gimbal to allow the propane stove to move with the motion of the boat and lit the burner. Then I tossed some butter in the frying pan that was locked in the grate of the cooktop. Once the butter melted, I dredged the fillets in flour and added them to the pan.

While the fish cooked, I checked the gauges. We were in no danger of running out of fuel, but we were running at less than a quarter charge on the batteries. I was worried about starting the engine or running the electronics. After breakfast, we could motor-sail and charge the batteries.

I went back to the galley and turned the fish. While it finished, I sliced up a melon, got two plates ready, and took them above.

"Here you go," I said, handing her a plate.

She jumped. "Wow, that looks great. *Gracias*," she said, her smile disarming me.

"*De nada*." I sat next to her on the port bench. My appetite got the better of me, and I quickly finished off the plate. She was still working on hers when I got up. "I'm going to start the engine. We need to charge the batteries."

"But it's so nice here, without all that noise," she said,

smiling at me. "Didn't you say that we wouldn't make any better time with it running? Maybe sit here with me for a while. We should get to know each other better."

I shrugged. "Just for an hour," I said, moving to the helm. My heart stopped when I pushed the start button and nothing happened. I tried again with the same result.

Working on the engine while underway was never something I looked forward to, knowing my reward, even if I fixed it, would be bloodied knuckles. She set her plate down, raised her skirt, and adjusted her top to allow the morning sun and my eyes access to her lines and her smooth copper skin, and I almost forgot the engine. A large roller shook me out of it. "I really need to check it. Even if we don't run under power, we need to charge the batteries."

I ignored her pout and went below, but not before seeing her strip off her top, exposing even more skin to the sun and my attention. The engine would be easier to fix once we hit the calmer bay waters, I rationalized, and went for her.

An hour later the fog lifted from my brain and we caught sight of land. "I really need to look at the engine," I said, breaking our embrace and checking the compass. Without looking back at her, because I knew if I did I might get distracted again, I went below and stacked the plates in the sink.

I dug the toolbox from the compartment under the bench seat and reluctantly went to the access panel. One at a time, I unbuckled the clips that held it in place and slid the cover back. I'd been through the engine once already to change the oil and filters, so I knew how it was configured. First I checked for leaks, and then I hit the remote starter. Nothing. I checked the wiring, looking for anything loose or corroded. It was all in good shape, and I sat back confused. I suspected there was no power getting to the solenoid and found a twelve-volt meter in the tool kit, which I used to confirm my prognosis. The problem was elsewhere, which made its resolution even harder.

Boat wiring was a constant plague. Loose wires, corrosion, and any multitude of fairies that owners suspected sabotaged things when they weren't looking, often made it impossible to diagnose a wiring problem, especially when under way.

"Any luck?" I heard her call down.

I slid the access panel back in place and climbed the stairs to get some fresh air. Rubbing the oil from my hands with a rag, I watched her steering topless in the sun. "Might want to get some clothes on. Land'll be coming up soon, and there's bound to be some fisherman looking at you instead of the water."

She laughed and started to dress. "So, what about the engine?"

"I suspect it's the wiring from the breaker panel to the starter. I'll never find it out here," I said.

"Is that a problem for us?" she asked, suddenly acting concerned.

"It'd be better to have it, but we can anchor offshore and . . ." I glanced behind the boat, realizing we had no dinghy. "Maybe it will be a problem."

Chapter 15

Losing the dinghy was not a problem in itself—the combination of no dinghy and no power was. On top of that, I was traveling on a US vessel not registered to me, without a passport, and with a Mexican woman I was not sure I could trust. I did have the document from Salvage Solutions that I was under contract to return the *Nai'a* to San Diego, but anyone with computer skills and a printer could have produced it. We would have been inconspicuous entering a port this size under power. The opposite was true trying to dock under sail. I needed a solution to get into port without power.

We were past the point and into the bay, both looking over the port rail at the city. "Can you take the wheel? I want to have a look at the charts," I said, waiting for her to grab hold before releasing control of the boat. The wind, which had remained constant since we had left yesterday, was now blowing close to twenty-five knots, and the rollers that had been so favorable were now steeper and closer together, making the going rough. I stumbled into the cabin and returned to the cockpit with the chart.

"Ever been here?" I asked her.

"No, but I bet he's over there somewhere," she said, pointing to the line of hotels in the distance. "Keeping a low profile is not in his genes."

I had the same thought and looked at the chart. There were

two harbors large enough to accommodate the *Dorado*. The closest was Nuevo Vallarta, which reminded me of the winding canals on the Florida coast. It appeared to be mostly residential. Further down the coast, right before the Zona Hotelera, was a larger harbor that was more commercial. The entrance was wide, and there appeared to be a large deep-water turning basin just inside the harbor. If it was as drawn, I should be able to sail in and drop anchor. The chart was not as detailed as I would have liked. The soundings were spaced far apart, and there were no hazards marked.

"Can you look something up on your phone?" I asked.

She gave me a questioning look. "I'm trying to save the battery if I can't charge it. What do you need?"

"Can you see if there is an online cruising guide or better information than this." I held out the chart.

"Sure," she said, pulling the phone from a pocket in her skirt and turning to the shade of the sail to see the screen better. "The signal is not very good, but here is something."

She handed me the phone just as a large wave picked us up and tossed us down its face. When I looked down at the screen there was an alert for a new message. It was in Spanish, but I could tell from the sender what it was: a confirmation of a bet from a sports-book site. All the questionable actions she had taken in the last two days now started to make sense. Every move she had made, probably including having sex with me, was designed to slow us down. She intended to profit from her sister's captivity. The message disappeared, and I tried to study the screen like I hadn't seen anything.

After what I thought was long enough, I handed it back to her. The aspect and size of the seas were pushing us farther off course with each wave that passed under us, and it took both hands on the wheel to wrestle the *Nai'a* back on course. I had to concentrate and steer each individual wave, but out of the corner of my eye I watched Marcella. The way she had arranged herself on the bench next to me might have looked innocent, until I tried to see the screen, which her body artfully blocked.

I watched her for a minute until she turned the phone off and put it back in her skirt. For the time being I had to put her subterfuge out of my mind and concentrate on the water ahead. A reef in the sails would have made it easier and more comfortable, and I wondered if I could trust her. Deciding to ride it out, I put everything out of my mind, something I excelled at, and concentrated on our course.

When we were within several miles of the harbor I passed the wheel to her, gave her the heading to steer, and went below to turn on the batteries. It was uncomfortable below with the hatches closed and the waves tossing the boat. I had to keep a constant hold on anything I could as I made my way to the control panel. I switched the battery selector to harness whatever power was left to both batteries and was about to go back up when I had a thought. If delay was her tactic, maybe she had disabled the engine. She could easily have gotten to the controls while I slept last night, and it wouldn't take any knowledge of boats to pull a wire.

I was about to look in the small compartment behind the battery switch when we hit another wave. My head slammed into the bulkhead and I knew whatever I suspected, and the repair if I was correct, would have to wait. We were destined to make the harbor under sail. Checking the growing knot on my scalp for blood, I climbed back on deck. More carefully than I would have a few minutes ago, I kept hold of the rail as I made my way to the helm and relieved Marcella. With the electronics working, I placed the cursor on the harbor entrance and pressed the go-to button. The GPS would now calculate our course over ground and give me a heading to steer. Without it, I would be forced to navigate by dead reckoning and take the chance of blowing by the inlet, a mistake that would require beating back into the wind and seas. Something

I wanted to avoid.

The seas had already pushed us past the point of no return, and although it looked like we would make the inlet on our current course, the electronics said otherwise, and I knew better than to argue with them. "We have to come about," I yelled over the wind.

A confused look crossed her face. We had practiced the maneuver several times in calm conditions. This was different. I would have to talk her through it. "Bring in the jib sheet as I start to come through the wind, then get the starboard line around the winch. It's going to happen a lot faster than we practiced."

I pointed the bow closer to the wind and waited while she brought the sail in. Despite my suspicions of her, I had to admire the way she had taken to sailing and got momentarily distracted watching her body move when she cranked the winch. Bringing my focus back to the boat, I scanned the rigging on deck to make sure there was nothing to ensnare either of us when the sails came over. We were ready.

"Prepare to come about!" I called over the wind.

"Ready," she called back.

I checked the compass, subtracting ninety degrees from our bearing, and spun the wheel. "Coming about!"

My nervousness disappeared as I watched her. Like she had done it a hundred times, she waited until the sail started to come over and released the line. With the agility of a cat she moved to the opposite winch and pulled the line taught, wrapped it twice, and started to crank. I kept one eye on the boat and the other on the compass as we settled onto our new course.

Although we were close hauled and beating into the wind and waves, the GPS said we were good. Noting the new bearing, I adjusted our course, and we sped toward the inlet. Marcella came back to the cockpit with a huge smile on her face. It was a shame I would have to watch her every move.

Half an hour later, we were a thousand yards from the inlet.

The course looked good, but I was hesitant to come in too hot. "We're going to bear off the wind slightly and furl the jib." I explained what I needed her to do. The wind was blowing so hard that even after I spilled wind from the sail, she still needed the assistance of the winch to bring the jib in.

Our speed dropped and I corrected course, pointing the bow at the rocky breakwater marking the northern entrance to the harbor, knowing the current would push us toward the center of the channel. The moment we crossed the imaginary finish line, the conditions changed and we coasted into the center of the basin. The wind was buffeted by the shore, leaving the water with only a light chop in the protected enclosure. Steering wide of center, I brought the bow into the wind, tightened the main sheet and locked it. Marcella was already on the foredeck, her bottom foot on the first stirrup, ready to guide the sail into its lazy jacks when I released the halyard.

Suddenly we were dead in the water, and I found myself in a deep embrace, enjoying the feel of her and forgetting the transgressions. A unique bond was forged by a trip like this, one I hoped would turn into something more, but first I had to figure some things out. I pried myself away from her and went forward. After releasing the safety, I used the remote windlass control to drop anchor and carefully manipulated the rode to the correct scope once I felt it grab. Without the luxury of an engine, we would be helpless if the anchor pulled and we drifted to shore.

The mood aboard quickly shifted. We looked at each other, the exhilaration of the past hour having faded. Not knowing what to do, instinctively we each sought our own space, something else I liked about our chemistry. She moved past the helm with her phone in hand, and I went below to see if my theory about the engine was right.

After opening the hatches and picking up the items tossed around by the seas, I found a light and brought it and the toolbox over to the battery bank. To ease any suspicions that I was on to her, I opened the access to the engine compartment as well. A woman's hand could easily have fit into the space above the switch, but it was too tight for me to see anything. Four screws later, the battery switch was removed and I shined the light inside the compartment. I first traced the heavy cables running to the batteries and found them intact. Next I moved to the smaller cable that ran to the engine, surprised to find it still attached.

I was starting to think I had misjudged her and was about to look back at the engine itself when I saw a thin wire hanging by itself. A quick glance at the switch found a vacant terminal connector. I removed the connector and, with a replacement I found in the toolbox, reattached the wire. I had no way of knowing if it had just happened or if it had been tampered with.

Chapter 16

I decided that this was no time to play games and went to the remote starter. There were more important things at stake. The engine fired right away, and I climbed the steps to increase the RPMs to charge the batteries.

"You fixed it," she said as I came up from the cabin.

I couldn't read her. "Loose wire. Happens all the time on boats," I said, pushing the throttle forward and raising the RPMs to charge the batteries. The engine was just loud enough to make it hard to talk over, and she returned to her phone, typing quickly, obviously in a conversation.

The decisions would be mine from this point forward, and the first order of business was to find Chuy before the authorities got suspicious of us anchored in the middle of the turning basin. After boarding us, the first thing they would ask for was my passport. With the RPMs hovering at twenty-two hundred, I hit the windlass switch. The motor strained for a minute, but as soon as the light anchor broke free, the rode came in easily. Once the hook clicked into place on the roller, I reversed to give us enough room to turn.

After we had glided back, I pushed the throttle forward and turned to the right, where I could see masts and antennas sticking above the seawall. "Can you find a chart of the harbor?" I asked Marcella. She barely acknowledged me and continued typing. Not wanting to get stuck in a dead end, I needed some information before entering the narrow channel. A minute later, she moved to my side holding the phone sideways. Several smaller channels were to the right, and a dozen finger piers jutted into end of the basin. They were all tight, and even with a slip reserved we would attract attention.

We passed a long pier with several Navy boats moored against it, and then a small river flowing into the channel caught my attention. Dropping to neutral, I sat in the opening studying the anchorage. A highway bridge was about a quarter mile in, its height limiting the access further inland. In front of the bridge I saw what I was looking for. Several older sailboats were anchored off a beach to the north. Unlike the white sand beaches of the ocean, it was dark and hard packed with small wooden fishing boats pulled on it. There was not enough money here for the authorities or the criminals to bother with the boats.

I turned into river's mouth and, aligning the *Nai'a* with the two other sailboats anchored there, maneuvered perpendicular to its flow. Pulling forward, I dropped anchor and reversed to set the hook. The stern ended up about ten feet from the beach. The other boats had anchors set on the hard-packed sand to keep them from swinging, but the *Nai'a* was ill equipped. Marcella was watching me, a look of concern on her face, but she remained quiet.

The next best thing to an anchor was a bucket, something most boats had. I found what I needed in the storage locker beneath the cockpit seat and tied a line to the handle with a bowline knot. "Time to get wet," I said, peeling my shirt off and sliding over the side with the bucket in my hand. "Can you hold onto the end of the line and tie it to the stern cleat?"

Halfway to the beach, my feet met the sand, and I was able to walk out of the water. With the bucket in my hand, I walked another dozen feet above the tide line and buried it in the hard sand. "Okay, pull it tight and tie it off," I called back to Marcella.

The line came tight, and I tested the holding power of the bucket. The heavy sand held it firmly. Satisfied, I returned to the boat.

The northern bank of the river would allow us land access to the marina, and, aside from having to get wet to gain the beach, we could check things out unobserved. I went first and she followed, attracting the attention of a group of fishermen repairing some nets by their boats. After checking the bucket anchor, I surveyed the beach.

"Stay here," she said and walked over to the fishermen. They immediately stopped their work and greeted her. They had a short conversation in Spanish, and she flashed her winning smile and turned back to me. I watched them watch her as she walked toward me.

"There are houses behind us. We can either walk upstream to the hospital and get the road there, or follow the beach around," she reported.

"Let's take the beach," I said, looking down at myself.

"Agreed," she said.

After a few minutes we found ourselves in a residential neighborhood, and, after stepping on the sidewalk, I wished I had brought my flip-flops. "He's not going to be in here," I said, looking at the estate style homes and feeling out of place in my board shorts. I looked over my shoulder for the security guard I expected to see any second.

She had left her phone onboard, not wanting to get it wet, but I remembered the layout of the harbor and started walking to the east, away from the water. We soon found ourselves on a commercial boulevard and turned left. The road seemed to be moving away from the water, and I was getting concerned when we came to a side street. Looking down it, I could see boats and we turned.

The road led us to the main marina. Staying to the shadows, we walked to the end of the road and looked out at the finger piers trying to locate Chuy and the *Dorado*. All the boats were large and expensive and it took a few minutes to identify his off to the right, tied up at a smaller pier by the marina office. It was more exposed than I would have preferred, but the sun would be down in an hour. I moved into the shade and found a bench where we could watch the boat.

We sat next to each other, but slightly farther apart than a couple would sit. We were quiet, each thinking our own thoughts, and I wondered how different our agendas were. Instead of planning a diversion to get them off the boat, I was more worried about a future relationship with a woman I knew I couldn't totally trust. Par for the course for me.

As if on cue, people emerged from the air-conditioned cabins of their boats for the sunset. All the boats except Chuy's. I checked my watch, realizing it was only an hour until the game started. If I had a plan, it would be time to implement it.

"What are you thinking?" she asked, guessing my thoughts.

"The game starts soon."

"It does," she said, sliding closer to me. "But think about this."

I looked at her, waiting for her to continue, knowing the next few sentences would dictate how I acted.

"With Marisa aboard, his guard will be down. She is safe as long as Gerardo does what he has been asked."

"Until the game's over. Then she is an inconvenience," I stated.

"So, we wait until halftime. That is when he will start celebrating," she said.

Her reasoning was solid, even if her motives were not. Chuy would likely be nervous and jumpy until he knew Gerardo was in his pocket for sure. "You're right. At halftime, we take out his cable and get them off the boat." The plan had just come to me. "He won't be able to resist, and I know the perfect place to send him.

I got up and she followed me back to the main street. On the corner was a boy with a handful of flyers. He had accosted us on our walk over, and I had glanced at the advertisement for a strip club. He saw us coming and approached. "Get him to go down to the docks and pass those things out. Make sure he hits Chuy's boat."

The boy approached and extended a flyer to me. Marcella reached out and took it, causing an embarrassed look on his face. He was about to run off when she called him. After a few terse exchanges, he headed down the side street to the docks.

"What did you say to him?" I asked.

"Just a little Catholic guilt."

We gave him a few minutes' head start and followed. The boy was doing exactly as she had asked, going boat to boat, handing the flyers to the people on deck waiting for the sunset. He reached the *Dorado* and dropped several over the transom. Perfect, I thought. Now I needed to figure out how to disable the cable.

The sun had just dipped below the horizon, and the decks quickly emptied. At once the sound of a sport commentator's voice could be heard from many of the boats—some in English and others in Spanish.

At tropical latitudes, twilight doesn't last long and it was soon dark. Several lights automatically came on, but this was still Mexico and they were infrequent, leaving many areas in darkness. I left Marcella on the bench and walked casually to an empty slip out of the light. There were pedestals set on the dock providing power, water, and, I was hoping, cable to the yachts. Reaching the first pedestal, I opened the hinged lid and looked at the hookups. There were two circuit breakers with large outlets below them for the shore power. Cutting the power was an option, but he would likely use his generators. Just below the outlets was the small coaxial connection I was looking for. Removing the rigging tool from my pocket, I tried to decide the best method to disable the jack. The marlinspike caught my attention. I opened the tool and looked at the horn-like device. The point fit into the jack, and, with a twist, I was able to pull the jack out. The knife would easily cut the wires.

"If I can get over there unobserved, we can cut the cable," I said after returning to the bench.

"So, we agree that we wait until halftime," she stated.

"Yes," I said, settling back to wait.

The chorus of TVs seemed to get louder, and I guessed the game had started. It was 7:15. Unlike most American sports, soccer used a running clock. I never quite got it, but the referees added time to the end of the game to compensate for delays. Halftime would be at exactly 8:00.

Chapter 17

"Better make sure the champagne's iced down," Chuy said while clipping the end off his second-half cigar. He placed the Cohibo Esplanido in his mouth and rolled it around, savoring the flavor before lighting it.

"Our boy's playing like a lovesick teenager," Frank said.

"I've got half a mind to bring his girlfriend up to watch his demise." Chuy pulled out a large butane lighter and paused while he rotated the cigar over the flame. "I wonder if those Mexican bastards will take his head off for this. Uncivilized sport."

"Look at that crowd," Frank said.

They sat in front of the big plasma screen in the salon, puffing on their cigars. The halftime commercials had just finished, and the producers were building the drama of the match by showing fights breaking out in the stands. *Gerardo* signs were already being taken and trampled. In the world of soccer, one bad half could threaten your career—a bad game, your life.

"What happened to that captain and the girls he was supposed to round up?" Chuy asked. He had purposefully delayed his party until he knew that Mexico's star was in the bag. Now, with the US up by two goals, he was confident. The Mexican star had not only been ineffective, the commentators were already questioning his decisions, blaming him directly for one of the United States' goals. He'd also gotten a yellow card, forcing him to play more conservatively or risk ejection.

"I'll go have a look," Frank said. He rose from the leather couch and went toward the sliding glass door, which he reluctantly opened, and went outside into the heat.

Chuy sat back, relaxing and dreaming of his return to the States. He wondered if his father would take him back as a son and restore his position in the family business. It would be touch and go on both counts. He knew the old man, and he would have to prove himself again. His patience would be tested until he could put his long-range plans into motion. Taking another sip of the aged rum, he puffed his cigar and rubbed his crotch impatiently. He was about to call for Frank when the screen went blank.

He jumped to his feet, spilling thirty-five-dollar cigar ash on his two-hundred-dollar Tommy Bahama shirt, and went to the door. The first thing he heard was the chorus of TVs coming from the other boats in the marina. Turning back to his boat, he saw the lights still on. He looked around and yelled for Frank and Roberto. Neither man answered and he went back into the salon. The TV screen remained jumbled with static. Moving to the unit, he carefully checked the connections. The cables seemed to be in place, and he stepped back and stared at the screen.

The sliding door opened and Roberto entered, "You called, *jefe?*"

Chuy looked at him and was about to ask about the girls when he saw several shapely figures through the smoked glass doors, giggling and dancing. "Goddamned cable's out."

"I will check it," Roberto said, opening the door. The girls must have caught the scent of air conditioning, money, or both, and barged into the salon.

"*Como estas, senoritas,*" Chuy said, smiling. Roberto had done well. He checked each of the three girls and could find nothing wrong with the man's choices. He was watching the back end of a brunette with an orange streak through her hair and a tight sequined dress bend over and pour drinks when he noticed the screen blink. The picture returned for a few seconds and then went back to static.

Regretfully he left the girls to their drinks and went outside to check on Roberto. After calling out several times, he saw Frank coming toward the boat. He approached and shrugged his shoulders in defeat. "No luck, boss," he said and climbed onto the deck. "I'm just the muscle. I don't know squat about this thing," he said, looking around the cockpit.

Chuy jerked his head at the cabin. Music was playing and the silhouettes of the girls dancing together were visible through the dark glass. "Well, go find him," Chuy said and turned to the door, but despite a stellar first half, he was too nervous to partake in the women. His life depended on the next forty-five minutes. "I gotta see the game. Maybe we can run someone off their boat or something," he said.

"No need," Frank said, leaning over and picking up a flyer from the deck. He looked at it for a minute and handed it to Chuy.

"Message from the gods," Chuy said. "Get the girls. We're going to Taboo."

* * *

The entire marina was watching the game, allowing me to sneak unseen to the shore power pedestal. Disabling the cable had been easy, but I feared anyone with any mechanical sense could patch together the wires. After unscrewing the female coax connector from the boat, I used the marlinspike to gouge out the male connector mounted to the panel. I walked casually to the end of the finger pier and turned onto the main dock, heading for the shadows, when I heard Chuy call out to his men, anger evident in his tone.

We had watched both men leave and thought about taking

the boat with just Chuy aboard. I already knew from firsthand experience that he had at least a shotgun aboard and wasn't afraid to use it, so we stayed back, waiting patiently for the plan to work. Roberto, the captain, had returned with three bar girls. Frank, the muscle, was still nowhere in sight.

Just after I had found Marcella and taken cover, the salon door opened and I saw two men on deck. A minute later, Roberto went to the flybridge, climbing down with what looked like a small toolbox. He stepped to the deck and climbed over the gunwale to the dock. I could see him clearly now as he approached the pedestal.

"We have to do something," I whispered to Marcella.

"Like what? I thought they had no TV," she said.

"That man is the captain. He can probably have that fixed in minutes," I said, seeing my plan unravel. Marcella had a blank look on her face. I wasn't sure if she didn't understand or if she was happy for the outcome. In either case, I didn't have time to analyze her motives—I had to act now.

Disabling the TV connection closer to its source would take too long. I would have to take on the captain. Physically, he was a larger and stronger man. I had nothing besides the rigging knife, but little knowledge of how to use it in a fight. What I did have was a beautiful woman. This would be a test of her motivations.

"You've got to distract him and get him away from that box," I said.

"Me?" she looked surprised.

"It's your sister aboard. I thought we were in this together," I said, playing every card I had.

I could see the turmoil in her eyes. They seemed to change color, but it was probably just the reflection when she moved her head to look at the man. She breathed out deeply and, without a word, rose and went to the finger pier. Checking my watch, I realized the second half was about to start, and once Gerardo was back on the field there was nothing anyone could do to change the outcome of the game.

"Let me have that tool thing," she said, extending her hand.

I handed her the rigging tool. She examined it and I watched as she compared the marlinspike to the knife, choosing the pointy tool for its length. Reduced to a spectator, I was curious as to how she was going to play this. I thought about moving closer to help her out if things went badly, but decided I would be more of a liability than an asset. This was going to be a test of feminine wiles against man's base instincts, and I had a pretty good idea which one was going to win.

She approached him and I saw the look of recognition in his eyes and then his mouth opened. She moved toward him quickly, but stopped suddenly. Both turned to a noise from the deck. She said something to him that I couldn't hear and walked swiftly back toward me, carefully keeping her face in the shadows. Reaching the bench, she sat close to me. Her breath came quickly.

"What'd you say to him?" I asked.

"Nothing," she said.

I had seen them talk, but didn't have time to question her now. Chuy, his muscle, and the three girls passed by the captain, who remained hunched over the box, working furiously to splice the wires. They ignored the man and continued toward the dock.

I had planned our observation post, or bench, as it was more commonly known, to the right of the finger pier, expecting them to take a left toward the main street and the club. Once they were well out of earshot I turned to her. "What do we do about him?" I asked.

"Don't worry about him," she said, shrugging her shoulders.

That was far from reassuring, but it was time. Rising from the bench, I walked toward the pier. Before committing myself, I looked down the main dock toward the city. There was no sign of Chuy's party. Turning back, Marcella was right behind me.

The captain looked up as soon as I set foot on the dock. As

confidently as I could, I walked past him to the boat. I couldn't be sure what, if anything, happened when Marcella passed. We reached the boat and I looked back at him, exchanging glances. A strange smile crossed his face. Without any indication of what he was up to, he got up and ran toward the main dock. Whether he intended to alert Chuy, the authorities, or just run away, there was nothing I could do about it now.

We boarded the boat quickly, and I ordered Marcella to the lines. I entered the salon and went down the short flight of stairs to the engine and mechanical rooms. Everything seemed in order, and I went back up to the main deck, checking the cabins one at a time. The last door I reached was locked. This must be the stateroom where Marisa was being held. She would have to wait until we were in open water. For now, I had to get us out of there.

I left the salon and climbed to the bridge. Glancing toward the dock, I checked for any sign of the captain or Chuy. Seeing no one, I fired up the twin engines. Looking down, I saw Marcella on the bow pulpit tossing the line toward the dock. Not wanting to waste time, I put the throttles in reverse and jumped down the ladder, freeing the stern lines from their pilings and climbing back to the bridge just as the boat eased out of the slip. I continued in reverse until she was clear and pushed down the throttles to a fast idle. I wanted out of there, but putting up a big wake was like setting off an alarm. I couldn't afford a run-in with the local authorities.

My heart was racing, and I fought the urge to push down the throttles until we reached the river mouth, where I glanced back and saw the *Nai'a* peacefully moored. I swore I would get back to her and turned forward. We were in the turning basin now, and I added a thousand RPMs. The boat reacted and pushed forward, leaving the harbor behind.

Chapter 18

We were in open water now and I started to relax. After the last few weeks on the sailboat, having this much horsepower underneath my feet was reassuring. With the throttles down, I kept the speed at a hair over thirty knots, trying to find the fine line between putting enough water between us and Chuy and conserving fuel. I was enjoying the ride. The flush of adrenaline from taking the boat along with Marcella by my side was exhilarating.

I set a westerly course to clear the bay, thinking about where to go. Chuy would automatically expect me to head north, back to the States. For that reason and the recovery of *Nai'a*, I started to bear southwest. I had traveled the coast before and knew several anchorages where we could hole up for a few days. Getting the two boats back up the coast by myself would be a problem. Holing up would give me some time to figure things out.

In the rush to escape, I had forgotten Marisa and wondered why Marcella hadn't been more concerned. Setting the autopilot to two hundred ten degrees, I eased off the seat and started for the ladder.

"Where are you going?" Marcella asked.

"Aren't you worried about your sister?"

The look on her face was clearly conflicted. I ignored her, not sure I wanted to hear her response, and climbed down the ladder to the deck. Entering the cabin, I went to the stateroom and looked at the lock. The mechanism had been removed and switched, placing the lock on the exterior. I knocked and turned the thumbscrew. The door opened and I looked into an empty room. Suddenly I saw movement behind the door and caught the arm as it came down to strike me.

I dodged her first blow, but she was quicker than I anticipated and caught me with a knee to the groin, causing me to double over in pain. Smashing her elbow down on my stooped back, I collapsed to the ground.

"I'm here to help you," I said meekly.

She took a step back, remaining in a fighter's stance, but allowing me to roll over. "Who are you?"

"Name's Will. I have your sister above, and we have taken the boat from Chuy," I started to explain.

"Marcella? What is that bitch doing here?"

Before I could respond, I heard a voice behind me.

"I'm here to help you, sister," Marcella said from the door.

The two women looked at each other, and I took the opportunity to gain my knees and then my feet. Using the cabin wall for support, I watched the interplay. Time seemed to suspend, illuminating each of their inner conflicts in the seconds before they embraced.

"It's about time you got here, or is it just in time," she said, looking at her designer watch.

"If you are all right, I need to get back to the bridge," I said, walking to the door.

"What about the game?" Marisa asked.

"It was halftime when we took the boat. Mexico was down two goals," I said. "Maybe we can get it on the radio up on the bridge."

"It is not too late," Marisa said.

"Too late for what?" Marcella asked, clearly concerned.

"To make this right," she answered, and followed me up to the bridge.

The radio was straightforward and I quickly found the game on one of the AM channels. The announcers were screaming and the crowd was roaring as if someone had scored and we huddled around the console waiting for details. Finally, the announcer recalled the scoring play, and, at minute sixty-five, Mexico had scored, making the score two to one in favor of the US.

The sisters' faces clearly reflected the spirits of the opposing fans. Marisa was happy, and Marcella, clearly not.

Marisa turned toward me. "I need a phone or computer."

Marcella turned away.

"Really, sister?" Marisa said. "Was all this a ruse to delay my rescue so you could make some money on the game?"

"Marisa gets this, Marisa gets that. Million-dollar house, billion-dollar boyfriend," she spat. "We are here, and you are safe," Marcella said. "Is that not enough?"

Marisa slid by me and swung a backhanded fist at Marcella. I dodged her and moved to the side. I had already felt her wrath. Stunned, Marcella dropped the phone and Marisa pushed her backward before reaching for it and immediately started working both thumbs, furiously typing messages.

"What are you doing?" I asked.

"Twitter and Facebook posts. Someone will see it and tell him I'm all right," she said.

"It is too late, sister," Marcella said, rising from the deck.

I watched Marcella from the corner of my eye as we returned our attention to the game. She was clearly nervous, but with every passing second, I could see the relief on her face. The game was at minute fifty-eight. With only two minutes remaining, the announcers were speculating about how much time would be added. I'd never gotten the concept of extra time, a subjective measure by all accounts of the cumulative delays in the game.

Both sisters were intent on the game, ignoring each other. My suspicions had been correct, but I felt a small degree of guilt as I watched Marcella biting her nails. No harm had come to her sister. She had not been involved in the kidnapping, only adding a slight delay to the rescue. I was kind of rooting for her.

The excitement had left the stadium when, with a minute left, the US intercepted a pass and moved the ball past midfield. The announcers described the movement of the ball, back and forth, with the US effortlessly killing the remaining time. Suddenly their tone changed. There was a flurry of activity on the Mexican bench and the coach received a warning to stay off the field. One of the defensemen must have heard him before he was removed to the sidelines and attacked the player with the ball, causing a stoppage in play with twenty seconds left. The announcers were focused on the activity on the Mexican sidelines as the defenseman was given a red card and ejected while the injured US player was helped off the field.

Time expired during the delay and the teams continued play, anxiously awaiting the decision about added time. Three minutes were announced, and the announcers could barely be heard over the crowd's displeasure. But in the interval something had changed, and the Mexican team appeared to be reinvigorated. Gerardo led the way, moving to steal the ball, only to have his pass intercepted. The two sisters, on either side of me, were spellbound.

Mexico stole the ball back and started charging toward the United States' goal, but the clock continued to tick. Several passes later, one of the announcers started counting down the remaining seconds. The tension radiated from the radio as he hit zero, but the teams continued to play. The referees must have added more time. Mexico passed twice more, the last to Gerardo in the center of the field. There was no time left, but as long as Mexico continued to drive, the referee would allow the game to continue. Gerardo pivoted and lost one defender, then passed to his right wing, who immediately returned the pass. Gerardo charged, dribbling around the last defenseman and, with the announcer screaming encouragement, booted a strong shot into the corner of the net. The crowd noise was all that was needed to tell the story.

* * *

Chuy brushed the girl's arm aside. "What the hell is going on here?" he screamed at Frank.

Gerardo had just scored the tying goal and the club was jubilant.

"Go back to the boat and see what his bitch has to say for herself," Chuy said, draining the contents of his champagne flute before slamming it on the table, breaking the stem. The game was headed to overtime, but the demeanor of the Mexican team and its star had changed. The girls sensed a change in their benefactor and huddled together in the back of the booth. Frank left the club and Chuy stared at the screen as the teams lined up for the first overtime period. He had a half hour to figure this out.

Less than a minute later, Frank was back at the table. Before Chuy could question him, he pushed Roberto in front of him. The captain had obviously never been in a club like this and alternated worried looks at Chuy with his fascination at the decadent surroundings.

"What?" Chuy asked him. "Stop staring at the freaking tits and tell me what's going on," he screamed over the beat of the music. One of the girls made a move to leave, but his look stopped her cold.

"The boat," Roberto stuttered.

"What about the boat?" Chuy said.

"*Jefe*, it is gone. A gringo and a woman took it," he said, with his head down in shame.

"You let this happen?" Chuy spat in his face.

"I was fixing the—"

"I don't care what you were doing," Chuy said and turned his attention to Frank. "Take this piece of shit and find a boat. We have to go after them."

"Right, boss," Frank said, moving toward the door and pushing a reluctant Roberto in front of him.

Chuy turned back to the TV, but he could tell by the atmosphere of the club that Mexico had scored again. His plans, his future, and his cash were slipping away with every tick of the game clock. There was no point in watching any longer. He got up, dropped a few hundreds on the table and steamed from the club. The marina was buzzing as the game entered the second half of overtime, with Mexico leading three to two. Time was his enemy now, and there was nothing he could do about it but seek revenge.

He reached the empty slip and saw Roberto and Frank in a heated conversation with a man by a large center console with three large outboards hanging from its transom. Walking over to them he realized the negotiations were not going well.

Moving between Roberto and Frank he studied the man. "What's the problem?" he asked.

"Is no problem, *señor*. These men want to use my boat. For a price, it is for rent," he said.

"Pay the man," he ordered Frank and walked down the finger pier to examine the boat.

"With what, boss? Whatever we had was on the boat. Bastard wants a grand a day."

Chuy looked at the man and reached into his pocket. He withdrew a handful of bills left from the club and realized he had spent the cost of a day's rental on cheap women and crappy champagne. The two hundreds and four twenties he had left were barely enough to fill one of the gas tanks.

"Give him the company credit card," Chuy spat.

"Must be cash, *señor*."

Chuy was about to blow, but turned and looked at the ground as the city seemed to erupt. It was obvious the game was over, and the outcome had put him in dire straits.

"Who was this man that took the boat?" he asked Roberto.

"I think it was the same one that was spying on us in Cabo. The girl, she looked familiar, too, like the one we had in the cabin," he said with his head down.

Chuy patted him on the back. There was no use scolding him any further. Somewhere in the next few days he would need him.

"You have a car that'll rent cheaper than the boat?" Chuy asked the man.

"Maybe, I have a brother," he said, eyeing the money in Chuy's hand.

Chapter 19

We were well out to sea and there were no boats on the horizon, at least none showing lights, when I slowed the *Dorado* to an idle. Running blind at night in foreign waters without a destination was not a good idea. I wanted to stop and rethink things. We were clear of Chuy, at least for now. I knew he would pursue, and I needed a plan to evade him and also to get the *Nai'a* back. The two sisters had reached some kind of agreement. Their behavior was inexplicable to me, but nurtured over thirty years together they had no need to speak their grievances.

The instrumentation was new to me and I took a few minutes to familiarize myself with the electronics. I flipped through the screens on the engine controls; fuel and oil showed full. Good news, because I had no idea when or where we would make port again. The displays were state of the art and showed all the necessary metrics, including fuel consumption.

"Can you get a signal?" I asked Marcella.

She was typing on her phone and ignored me.

"Are you going to answer?" Marisa scolded her.

The last thing I wanted was another fight between these two. "This is a Hatteras sixty-four. I need the fuel capacity," I told her, hoping that if it were stated as an order she would comply.

She shifted slightly and nodded.

While she looked up the specs, I started up the radar. The

five- and ten-mile rings were empty of boat traffic. Zooming out to twenty miles, I could see some activity near shore as well as what I assumed were longline fishermen working farther offshore. The chart plotter started and beeped when it acquired our position. I scanned the screen looking for a hole to hide in. Boca de Tomatlan caught my eye. A river fed the small bay and it looked like there was a good sheltered anchorage. Changing course to the east, I placed the cursor just outside of the bay and hit the go-to button. The autopilot took over the controls and I sat back to think.

Taking the two boats back up the coast could be done, but the thousand-mile tow would be difficult in good weather and dangerous in bad. I would have to plan weather windows and anchor more often than I would prefer. I would be conspicuous with the sportfisher towing the sailboat and would certainly have to deal with the authorities. Without a passport, that might be a problem. I looked over at the two sisters and wondered what to do about them.

Neither seemed to notice or care about the change in course, and I went down to the salon to have a quick look around before we reached the bay. Weapons might be useful, and cash was going to be a necessity. When I had left California, I had been prepared to pay off the dock fees on the *Nai'a* and sail her home. I had nowhere near the cash to pay the fuel bill to bring the *Dorado* back. Salvage Solutions would help out, but that would require sitting in port and having funds wired. Without my passport, that was a bad idea.

There was nothing of use in the salon, unless I found a market for expensive cigars and liquor. Moving forward I checked the staterooms. The bodyguard's cabin was utilitarian, and after a quick search I found several boxes of .38-caliber bullets but no gun. If he had a weapon, it was on him. I moved toward the master stateroom. Chuy had spread himself out, and, from the looks of things, was used to a maid. Clothes were scattered on the floor and bed. I waded through the mess and searched the nightstand, where I found a roll of hundreds, bound drug-style, with a rubber band. Opening it up, I quickly counted five thousand. I would have to sit down to do the math, but it sounded like enough to get me home.

I heard the GPS beep and ran back to the bridge. Lights from the small fishing village were visible ahead, and I took control back from the autopilot and steered toward the wide bay. With the help of the electronics, I was able to find a good anchorage in twenty feet of water near two shrimp boats. I pulled back the throttles, allowing the boat to drift to a stop and not disturb our neighbors, then I hit the windlass switch. The rattle of the chain startled me and woke Marcella, who was sleeping on the settee. The anchor splashed and I counted to twenty, figuring that was about a hundred feet of rode, plenty of holding in shallow water on a calm night.

I killed the electronics and shut down the engines. Before heading down, I looked at the women again, both asleep like cats. Leaving them, I went below, took one look in Chuy's stateroom, and decided on the couch. It was a long time since I had slept, but it still took me a while to wind down. I thought about taking a shot of Chuy's high-dollar rum. Somewhere in that decision, I passed out.

* * *

"This piece of crap for two hundred!" Chuy screamed at the beat-up car, kicking the tire in anger. "Where the hell is this thing going to get us?"

Frank went to the driver's seat and took the keys the man had given him. "Where to, boss?"

"The hell if I know. They're out in the freakin' ocean. A whole lot of water this thing can't get to," Chuy spat.

Roberto cleared his throat.

"You got something to add?" Chuy stared him down.

"If I may. That fancy boat has radar. We don't need to use the boat to see where they have gone," Roberto said.

"Brilliant. Why didn't you think of that?" Chuy asked Frank, not really knowing what Roberto was talking about.

"The transponder is gone, of course, but there aren't many boats that size this time of night," Roberto said.

They left the car and went back to the dock. The streets were alive with people pouring in and out of the restaurants and bars. The festivities were in full swing, celebrating Mexico's victory. Chuy tried to ignore them and focus on the task at hand. The boat was all he had left, and the woman aboard and her boyfriend were going to pay for this.

There was no one around when they reached the boat. "Probably took my two bills to the closest bar," Chuy said.

"*Jefe*, we don't need the man," Roberto said, stepping aboard the center console. He went to the helm and lifted the cover protecting the electronics. "The batteries are on. This will only take a few minutes."

"Good man," Chuy said, and paced the dock. "When I find that two-bit whore, there's gonna be hell to pay."

The electronics had completed their start-up sequence and Roberto was busy working the displays.

"You know what you're doing?" Chuy asked, hopping down to the cockpit and looking over his shoulder.

"*Si*. They took off less than an hour ago. That gives them a maximum range of forty miles." He zoomed the radar out to show four rings. "Each ring is ten miles."

There was nothing in the outer ring and two boats in the third. "Which one is ours?"

"Neither of those. They are fishing boats." He moved the cursor to the south and zoomed in on a moving dot. "That is it."

"You sure?" Chuy asked.

"Without the transponder, there is no way to be sure, but the signal matches the size of the boat, and they are making for Boca de Tomatlan. If I were to hide, that would be a good place."

"You're all right," Chuy said, slapping Roberto on the back.

The captain breathed deeply, turned off the electronics, and replaced the cover. "If you no longer need me . . ."

"Not so fast. You've been very helpful, and I expect there will be more need for your skills before this is over."

Roberto was about to protest when he felt the prick of a knife in his side.

"*Si, jefe*. Whatever you need of me," he said.

They climbed back onto the dock and went to the car. "What's the name of that town?" Chuy asked Roberto.

"Boca de Tomatlan."

"Got that, Frank? Put it in your phone and let's get down there. We've got some unfinished business to take care of."

The engine protested but finally started. The car bucked as Frank backed out of the parking space and then lurched forward. It took a few miles for him to get the feel of the worn-out clutch, and they were soon barreling down Mexico 200. "Says it's only twenty miles," Frank said, glancing at the screen.

The car bounced. "It's Mexico. That could be a day and a freakin' half on these roads," Chuy said. He opened the window to get some air and looked at the city, alive with victory around him. After a few miles, the road became dark and started following the coast. It wasn't a straight shot, but nowhere near as bad as he expected, and forty-five minutes later they saw the lights of a village ahead. "That it?"

"Not yet." Frank fumbled with the phone and hit the narrow shoulder. "Damned roads are made for goat carts."

"Lemme see that phone," Chuy said, taking the phone from the armrest. He set down the revolver that the owner had thrown in for another fifty bucks. He had been trying to clean it with a dirty rag, with little effect. Between bumps he studied the map. "Almost there." He studied the dot moving along the lone road. They left the town and traveled what he thought was about five miles. The road took a hairpin turn and he saw lights ahead. "That's it. Looks like this road runs next to some kind of harbor. What do you think, Roberto?" He handed the phone back.

Roberto took it carefully. "*Si, jefe*. If it were me, that's where I would go." He handed the phone back to Chuy.

They entered the town a few minutes later. "Pull in there," Chuy ordered.

Frank parked and the three men left the car, heading toward a restaurant with a view of the harbor. They walked around the small building to the beach. The harbor was quiet, with only three boats anchored. "There she is," Chuy said, pointing to a dark shape.

"What's the plan, boss?" Frank asked.

"We gotta take them right now, when they least expect it. That bitch is probably still aboard, too. If we wait until tomorrow, it'll be too late." He looked down at the beach. A row of wooden fishing boats was lined up above the tide line. The dim light of a small fire caught his eye, and he saw a handful of men sitting on crates, drinking beer.

"There's our ride," he said.

Chapter 20

Chuy approached the group of fishermen on the beach. They looked up at him with smiles on their faces, either from the beers they had drunk, the result of the game, or more likely both. The mood changed when he pushed Roberto in front of him, then lifted his shirt to show the gun in his waistband. What he had seen when he stripped down the weapon on the ride over gave him no confidence it would fire. The revolver was in desperate need of oil and a thorough cleaning. The threat would have to be enough.

The men rose and moved backward. Roberto motioned to Chuy to stay back and went toward them with his hands out to show he was unarmed. Talking as he approached, they loosened up a bit. One man finally stepped forward. He and Roberto went to one of the boats, had a look at it, and returned to Chuy.

"It is in good shape," Roberto said.

"They all look like crap," Chuy said, scanning the row of boats on the beach.

"The engines are new, *jefe*," Roberto said, pointing to the new outboards mounted to the old wooden transoms.

"Some salesman had a field day with this village. They probably pay more in interest than they catch in fish," Chuy said, walking toward the man's boat. "He'll take the deal?"

"*Si*, he is willing to wait until you can get the money back from your boat," Roberto said.

"Smart man," Chuy said, kicking the hull. "You sure this thing floats?"

"These are good boats, *jefe*. Not like yours, of course, but seaworthy."

"Let's roll then, before that bastard smokes the rest of my cigars." He turned to Frank. "Stay here with the car and keep your phone on. I'll be in touch in case they slip us."

The fisherman called to his friends. An old truck axle was rolled out and placed in front of the bow. Several of the men lifted the boat while two others placed the dolly underneath the hull. The men gathered at the transom and stared out to sea.

"What are they doing?" Chuy asked.

"You count the swells. It looks like four big ones and then a lull. We will go after the next set," Roberto said.

Chuy couldn't see the difference. Finally one of the men called out, "*Uno, dos, tres.*" Together they lifted the stern and pushed the boat toward the water. The bow entered and two men pulled the wheels back while the fisherman and Roberto hopped aboard.

"I gotta get my feet wet? These are thousand-dollar Italian loafers—shit," Chuy complained.

"*Vamanos!*" the fisherman called.

His urgency got Chuy moving. With a pained look on his face, he ran through the foot of water and jumped aboard. The fisherman was at the stern with the motor already running. The second Chuy was aboard, he gunned the engine and two hundred horsepower pushed the boat toward the breakers. The fisherman had timed it perfectly, and the boat crested the first big wave before it broke, then slid down its back and was in open water. The surf was behind them now, and the fisherman steered a large circular course to avoid some unknown peril, then pointed the bow at the *Dorado*.

Chuy made a slicing motion across his throat. "Tell him to

idle," he said softly. "We need a little stealth here."

Roberto relayed the information and the engine quieted. Slowly they approached the sportfisher. There was no sign of a lookout or any action aboard. In fact, the boat looked dead. "Have him ease her up to the transom," Chuy said.

The roar of the big engines startled them and then the *Dorado* started to back down, missing the wooden fishing boat by less than a foot. The larger boat spun and moved forward. It seemed to pause, but the minute they heard the anchor break the surface of the water it accelerated. Chuy was beyond mad and, without thinking, pulled the revolver and fired all six chambers at the fleeing craft.

* * *

The small village was so quiet that, besides the constant breaking of the surf on the beach, every sound woke me. I was just about asleep again, after the last false alarm, when I heard the distinct sound of an outboard throttle down. I swung my legs to the deck and, without turning on any lights, moved carefully out the salon door and up to the bridge. I stood with my back to the wheel, scanning the water and wishing I had taken the time to back into the anchorage for an easier escape. The faint light from the rising moon highlighted the dark water, but it was still too low in the sky to help me see. Rollers worked toward shore undisturbed, their sound loud enough to cover an outboard at idle.

Thinking it was another false alarm, I started to climb down the ladder when something to the west broke the pattern of the waves. It was a small fishing boat heading directly toward us. I had no idea if Chuy had somehow found us or if it was the local customs agents, and I cursed myself for not putting out the yellow quarantine flag. The signal would have at least told any observer that I intended to visit the office in the morning. Whoever it was, I couldn't risk it and started the engines. The second they caught, I hit the windlass switch, and, before waiting for the rode and anchor to come aboard, I backed and cut the wheel, just missing the boat.

I could clearly see four men, and my eyes met Chuy's. They held for a long second. As I saw the dull glint of steel pointing at me, I slammed the throttles into forward and cut the wheel hard to starboard. One of the women stuck her head up, and I yelled to keep down when I heard gunfire over the throaty roar of the big diesels. For once, it was nice to be on the larger horsepower side of the equation and the boat took off. I steered into the dark night, straight out to sea. Daring a look back, I saw the small boat, up on plane chasing us, but it was a futile effort—they would never catch us.

Out of habit, I looked down at the gauges and realized that something was wrong. The temperature on the port engine was climbing into the red zone. The women were up with me now, both looking back at the boat behind us. It was surprisingly fast, and I looked at the GPS. Our speed was over forty knots. I doubted even with a new engine the old wooden boat could top thirty. We were a quarter of a mile ahead when I dropped RPMs by a quarter, hoping this would match their speed and give me time to figure out what was wrong. An alarm interrupted my thoughts and the port engine shut down.

"Marcella, take the wheel and keep the course on three hundred," I said. The huge V hull was slicing effortlessly through the waves that I hoped were pummeling the smaller boat. "Marisa, keep watch. I'm going down to the engine room and see what's wrong." I looked at the women to see if they understood and got a scared look from both. Whatever their past agendas, we were now in this together with a common enemy.

Climbing down the ladder, I paused on the deck and looked around for any damage from the gunfire. There was nothing evident, and I went through the salon to the small flight of stairs that led to the engine room. I knew something was wrong as soon as I opened the fire door and a blast of hot air hit me. Propping the door open, I entered the sauna-like room and looked at the controls. The gauges told me what I suspected, but not the cause. The starboard engine was in the normal range, but the port engine had overheated and shut down. I checked for oil or water leaks, but found none. There was nothing else I could do here and left the room, leaving the door ajar to dissipate some of the heat. I went back on deck, leaving the salon door open for ventilation, and stared back at the dark seas. The moon had risen and hung an inch over the horizon, reflecting the crest of each wave, but still offered no real light.

It took a few minutes scanning the dark water to locate the fishing boat still hanging a quarter mile behind. It was keeping pace. Climbing to the bridge, I was assaulted by questions, which I didn't have answers to. To deflect them, I buried my head in the gauges and chart plotter. Running on one engine in a boat designed for two was not a good situation. The efficiency and speed came from the synchronization of the twin propellers. With only one engine, we were running at less than half speed.

I turned my attention to the chart. The only option I could think was to run them out of fuel, and this meant heading south or out to sea. Unsure of the problem with the engine, I was reluctant to head out of sight of land and chose the barren southern coast. La Manzanilla was the closest city with any kind of services, and I expected it was out of their range.

"We are heading to La Manzanilla, where you both can get off. They should run out of fuel by then, so it should be safe," I said as confidently as I could. I still had not pinpointed the problem with the engine and, even if I did, was not sure I could fix it while we were underway. They both moved as one to the bench seat and started talking to each other. From a quick glance, it appeared this was more a strategic than emotional conversation.

Methodically, I looked ahead, then at the plotter to check position, then at the gauges to monitor the starboard engine, and finally behind; each item was critical to our escape. Miles passed and nothing seemed to change. The fishing boat held a quarter mile back, and the starboard engine was still in the green. It had been roughly an hour since we had left the harbor, approximately half the distance to La Manzanilla. There was no way of knowing how much fuel they had left, but figuring eight gallons an hour, they might make it. Somehow we needed to increase speed.

"Take the helm," I called to Marcella.

She came toward me, positioning herself with her hip against me and reaching across the wheel so her breasts rubbed against my arm. I couldn't help but notice the change in body language, but this was not the time to worry about motives. I gave her the course and dropped down to the deck. Once more, I checked the engine room. It was still dry, and I tried to think of the source of the problem. It could be a number of internal problems, but the boat had run well before we left the harbor. The change had happened then, and I remembered the gunshots.

Leaning over the port side I tried to find the intake that brought raw water in to cool the engine. It appeared to be free of debris, and I turned my attention to the outlet, which was spraying water like a high-pressure sprayer instead of a garden hose. Something was wrong, and I suspected one of the bullets had mangled the outlet, decreasing the water flow and causing the engine to overheat. Without better light, I couldn't see the extent of the damage. The risk of showing our position was not worth the reward of seeing what I likely couldn't fix now. Knowing what it was helped, and I went back down to the engine room to see if I could find a solution.

Chapter 21

After working on the sailboat's engine, I was overwhelmed at the size and industrial look of the *Dorado's* engine room. It was well lit, allowing plenty of space to work on the large diesels occupying each side of the room. It was not at all what I was used to. I found the port where the heated water discharged and looked at the swollen hose in alarm. The rubber tubing was rated for high temperature at a low pressure. It had been pushed to its extreme and was near the point of bursting. The engine had shut off just in time.

The room had no windows, but it was bright and painted a glossy white, which reflected the light. I traced the route of the hose to a small crawl space below the deck to where it exited the boat. Squeezing in the narrow space, I contorted my body to reach the fitting, which terminated at a seacock.

I had an idea how to fix the problem, at least temporarily. A permanent repair would need parts. Chuy would be on us in less than a minute if we stopped, making a repair while underway a necessity. Running at twenty-four knots was economical with both engines. With only one, running full out, our fuel consumption would skyrocket. Unless I could increase our speed, they would stay on our tail until one of us was forced to stop for fuel—and which one ran out first was now a crapshoot.

I went back up to check our course and tell the women what

I had in mind. Climbing to the bridge, I found the sisters sitting side by side at the wheel. "I found the problem. The raw water discharge from the engine took a hit and is partially clogged. The only thing we can do is connect another hose to the outlet at the engine and run it overboard." From the way they looked at me, I was not sure they understood what I was saying.

"It should be pretty simple," I said, trying to reassure them, knowing full well that even the simplest tasks were difficult while underway. I turned around to locate the fishing boat. We were locked on each other, neither giving nor gaining an inch. "We're stuck in a bad spot without knowing how much gas they have."

They both looked at the boat behind us. The moon was now a quarter way through the sky, finally casting enough light to see our pursuit. It was reassuring to know exactly where they were, but they could see us as well.

"I can help," Marisa said.

"Always the hero," Marcella replied too quickly.

Marisa ignored her and looked at me. I nodded and followed her below.

"It's going to take all three of us to get out of this," I said to Marcella before dropping to the deck.

She ignored me. My feet hit the deck and I stopped in the cockpit, where Marisa was digging through the storage lockers. "You know she likes you," she said.

"What are you looking for?" I asked, dodging the question.

"Some hose or tubing to run the water out. You can't ignore it," she said, steering the conversation back where she wanted it.

I moved to the gunwale and showed her the raw water wash-down hose. "I can't figure it out either," I said.

"You two are good together," she said. "She's never had a man that could take care of himself. I think that is why she makes some bad decisions."

I ignored her. "This should do it," I said, changing the

STEVEN BECKER

subject and climbing down to the engine room. In a corner was a small tool chest with several drawers. I found a 5/16" wrench and a flat-head screwdriver and moved to the discharge port, where I set the tools and the female end of the hose. We were side by side in the small hot room and I could feel her next to me. There was something about her, maybe the calm assurance, or the fact that she was unavailable, that made me comfortable around her. Working together, we ran the other end of the hose out the door to the deck, and then returned below.

"Ready?" I asked.

She nodded.

My "simple" statement came back to bite me sooner than I expected. After removing the swollen hose, I examined the barbed fitting and cut the end off the wash-down hose. Setting it in place with the hose clamp over it, I realized the diameter was smaller than the other, and I had to slit the hose to get it over the fitting. Twice I skinned my knuckles trying to work the wrench over the small nut before it was finally secure—or at least I hoped it was.

"Tell her to start it up," I said to Marisa.

A minute later, the engine turned over.

Water started to flow through the hose, and I thought we were home free. I could feel the boat accelerate and turned to the fitting, only to be hit by a high-pressure stream of water.

Moving out of the spray, I looked at the fitting. As long as the hose held, only a fraction of the water was leaking, but the engine was not up to speed yet.

"Tell Marcella to bring it up so the RPMs are the same," I called to Marisa, who was waiting outside the door.

"Are you alright?" I heard her ask.

"Yeah. Just tell her."

The engine changed tone as she accelerated, and with it so did the spray. Everything in the room was wet, and I saw water start to rapidly accumulate on the floor. I turned to leave the room, satisfied that the repair would hold, when something hit me in the head hard with enough force to knock me from my feet.

Water was everywhere and I could feel it pooling beneath me. I felt the back of my head where the hose had struck me and my hand came away with blood. I crawled to the door.

"Will!" Marisa yelled.

I waved her away and crawled on my hands and knees across the threshold. "Close the door," I told her and collapsed on the deck.

The echoes from the engines pounded through my head and I felt hands grab me. I opened my eyes and thought I was seeing double. Both sisters were swarming over me. "I'm okay."

"Your head is bleeding," Marisa said, holding a towel against the wound.

"We have bigger problems than that," I said. My voice sounded almost normal now and the pain was subsiding. With their help, I gained my feet and, after wobbling for a few steps, found my balance and staggered through the door to the deck.

I looked back at our wake. We now had enough speed to lose the fishing boat, but we were slowly sinking. With water flooding the engine room, the bilge pump was the only thing keeping us afloat. The other problem was if the water rose to the level of the electronics in the engine room, it could easily short a sensor or control and we would be dead in the water.

"Let's increase speed to forty knots and find someplace we can hole up in and figure this out," I said. Marcella understood and climbed to the bridge. I felt the RPMs increase and almost fell to the deck as the boat surged forward. It was reassuring to feel the engine noise rise an octave as the boat sped forward. I felt our course change a minute later. We might as well take advantage of our speed while we still had it and lose the fishing boat.

"I need to look at your head," Marisa said.

I felt a warm trickle of blood run down my neck and

followed her into the cabin.

"Relax, I will take care of you," she said.

I sat down and tried to smile, but I was seeing double again. "I'll live. First we need to get the door to the engine room open and let the water out." It made sense that by opening the door, water would pour out into the adjacent areas, allowing the level to drop before it did any damage to the engines. "Have a look and see if you can reach it without standing in the way."

She handed me a towel, went down the stairs, and returned a minute later. "I think I can get it with a pole or something," she said.

Above us were a dozen heavy trolling rods, neatly spaced in a carved mahogany holder. "One of those work?" I asked.

She pulled one down and went back to the stairs. I could see her back as she manipulated the rod to unlatch the door. Suddenly she screamed and jumped back. I could hear water flooding out of the room. "Are you okay?" I tried to get up, finally reaching my feet when she emerged from the opening.

"Just scared me. That's a lot of water," she said, catching her breath.

"How high is it?"

She peered back down the stairs. "About to the top of the first step," she said.

"We'll have to keep an eye on it. Can you run up to the bridge and make sure the temperature is back to normal and see if we've put some distance between us and the fishing boat?" After she left, I started to move, slowly at first, trying to figure out what worked and what didn't.

"They are falling back and the engine temperature seems normal. There is a bay about forty miles down the coast that we are heading to," she said, coming toward me. "No more excuses. Let me take care of you."

I sat and succumbed. "Just check the water every few

minutes."

She turned the cabin lights on and positioned me underneath them. Opening the first aid kit, she removed a suture kit. "This is going to hurt," she said, and started rubbing the back of my head. Once it was clean, she started sewing the wound closed. I jumped every time she pushed the needle through my skin, but it was reassuring that I could feel it.

"It will work for now," she said, cleaning up the mess.

"Thanks, I think. Can you check the water level?" I asked.

"It's up to the second step now!" she called out in alarm.

The bilge pumps were not keeping up. I felt lightheaded when I rose, and did my best to hide it. Marisa must have noticed and came by my side. "Help me up to the bridge."

Climbing the ladder to the bridge brought a whole new level of pain and I thought I might pass out. Finally I gained the platform and crawled to the helm. After several breaths, I struggled to the seat and, with stars in my eyes, scanned the instruments. The temperature was reading normal and the speed was just over forty knots. I looked behind us for the fishing boat. Its low profile made it invisible at this distance. Adjusting the radar, I found them, now a half mile behind us, dropping back, but still following. The cove was now thirty miles away, far enough that we could put enough distance between us that they wouldn't see where we went. It was also far enough away that I had to worry we might sink before we reached safety.

Chapter 22

"Can you see the bastards?" Chuy yelled at Roberto.

"No, *jefe*. They increased speed a half hour ago and are out of sight."

Chuy scanned the water in front of them, seeing nothing that looked like a boat. "They changed course before we lost them. Does he know where they were headed?"

Roberto huddled with the driver. "He does not know this coast and is also worried we will run out of gas."

"There had to be something wrong with the boat for them to be going that slow. That sucker 'll cruise almost twice that fast. Follow the last course they were on. We'll get to land, get some gas, and figure it out," Chuy said.

Roberto went back to the fisherman, who appeared satisfied with the plan. Chuy ducked down below the gunwales and pulled out his phone, shielding it from the spray. He went to his contacts and pressed Frank's name.

"We lost them," he shouted into the phone when the bodyguard answered. The reception was cutting in and out, making conversation difficult.

"There ain't shit on this coast, boss," Frank said. "I've been driving for hours."

"There's something wrong with the boat and they changed course toward shore before we lost them. Find a map and get back to me. The *pescadoro* running this boat doesn't know where we are," Chuy said.

"I'm in this town called La Manzanilla. First thing I found down the coast. I got just one bar of cell service. I'm surprised you got me. Wait. There's a coffee joint that should be open soon. Maybe they have Wi–Fi."

Chuy looked at the horizon in front of them and could just make out a thin line of land in the predawn glow. He tried the maps app on his phone, but there was no Internet connection. With nothing to do but wait, his rage built as his body was jarred by every wave they crashed through. He scanned the water in front of him, hoping for a sign of where the boat had gone. Revenge would be had, but not before he got retribution. That pompous soccer star had cost him a million dollars. If he wanted his girlfriend back, we would have to write that check—plus interest.

The coastal hills were featureless, backlit by the rising sun as they approached land. Several small islands rose out of the sea in front of them, guarding the entrance to a small bay. They were still too far away to see if there was a town, and he checked his phone again, finding no service at all—not a good sign. A few minutes later, the fisherman steered past the first seamount and entered the shallow water. The only sign of civilization was a sailboat anchored in the lee of a smaller island.

"There ain't shit here," Chuy yelled to Roberto, his voice suddenly loud as the fisherman eased off the throttle. The boat sank back in the water and moved slowly toward the mainland. "What's he doing?"

"He will beach the boat and find gas," Roberto said.

"Bullshit he will. We ain't doin' the whole Mexican thing and take a day and a half to find gas." That was not going to work. Chuy looked at the sailboat. "Tell him to head over there," he said, pointing to the sailboat and pulling the rusty revolver out of his waistband. He opened the cylinder and spun it. The chambers were all empty. With no ammunition, he would have to bluff whoever was on the boat.

The fisherman skillfully kept the bow of his small boat ten feet off the stern of the sailboat. "Hey!" Chuy yelled across the water. He had already seen activity in the cabin. "We are in trouble and need some gas," he said, eyeing the jerry cans strapped to the safety rail.

"Ahoy." A man emerged, rubbing the sleep from his eyes.

Chuy searched the boat, wondering if he was alone. "Morning," he said, his voice calm. "You alone?"

The man ignored his question. "What can I do for you?" he asked warily.

"We need some gas, is all," Chuy said, scanning the boat for any sign of trouble.

"I can help you out with a few gallons. There is a town down the coast. I'll give you enough to get there," he said.

"That's very helpful, however, we will need whatever you have," Chuy said, becoming impatient and raising the gun. "Roberto, tell him to bring the boats together and grab those cans," he ordered.

The man was backing toward the cabin with his hands up when Chuy saw the barrel of the shotgun emerge from the cabin. The shape of a woman could be seen behind it. She passed the gun to the man and disappeared. "I'm happy to help out with a few gallons," the man said firmly. "We can keep this friendly."

Chuy bit his tongue, trying to control his anger. No one dictated terms to him. "Thanks. We'll just pull up to you then," he said, lowering the gun.

The man relaxed and dropped the barrel slightly. "You can stay there." He backed toward the first can and, with the shotgun secured in the crook of his arm, untied the lashings and brought it to the transom.

The fisherman started forward to take the can. Chuy signaled him to stay where he was and went forward to make the exchange. "I'll do this myself," he said, moving toward the bow. The boats were only feet apart, and the man leaned the gun against the gunwale and waited.

The two boats were just about touching now, and the man leaned over the side with both hands on the can. He was vulnerable and Chuy feinted as if he was going to take the can. Instead of grabbing the handle, he reached up, grabbed the man's shirt, and pulled him into the water. He ignored the muffled scream from the cabin and reached over for the shotgun.

"Come on out here where I can see you," he called out. Slowly the woman emerged from the cabin with her hands in the air. "Roberto, hop on over and get those cans." He held the gun on the woman. "Just stay where you are and everything is going to be fine," he called to the man treading water a few feet away.

Roberto passed the four five-gallon cans across to the fisherman, who stashed them by the transom, and hopped over to the smaller boat. The fisherman went back to the helm and backed away from the sailboat. Chuy waved at the couple as they pulled back. The fisherman turned and pointed them toward open water. Chuy checked the shotgun, emptying the six shells and reloading them with a smile on his face.

* * *

We limped into the bay and anchored among several sailboats. The handful of ibuprofen I had taken took the edge off my headache, and I seemed to be regaining my balance. When I was sure the hook was set, we sat on the bridge.

"We need to keep watch and monitor channels sixteen and seventy-two on the VHF as well. A meal would probably be a good idea too. I'm going below to fix the discharge," I said and carefully descended the ladder to the deck. A quick look over the side confirmed that the bilge pumps were running. With the engine off, they would take care of the water. Returning to the engine room, I looked past the blood spot on the wall where I had hit my head and waded through the two feet of water to the hose.

First I would try to rig the temporary hose so it would hold, in case we had to make a fast exit, then I would go overboard and see if I could fix the damage that Chuy's bullet had caused. It was very different working without the rolling seas and the running engine, and I had the temporary hose rigged in a few minutes. I figured I'd give it a test and then see about the permanent fix when I smelled bacon cooking in the galley and realized it had been the better part of a day since I had eaten.

Chuy's pantry was well stocked, and Marcella was cooking pancakes and eggs to go with the bacon. I sat down and watched her, admiring her efficiency. She noticed me, turned around and smiled. "How're you feeling?" she asked.

"Better," I said, continuing my report, "the bilge pumps will handle the water, and I have a temporary fix for the engine."

She nodded approval and went back to work. I grabbed a piece of bacon, remembered that I was going to test the engine, and went back to the bridge. After giving Marisa the same update, I started the engine, left it in neutral, and went back down below. The water was receding and I couldn't detect any leaks. Back on deck, the discharge was running from the hose. After breakfast, I would see about making the permanent repair.

Breakfast was quickly devoured. Marcella was a good cook, another asset added to the growing list of things I liked about her. Now, if only I could trust her. We ate on deck, with an eye to the open water, but there was no activity besides a few local fishing boats trolling around the seamount just offshore.

"I'm going overboard to have a look at the discharge," I said, and went toward the cabin.

"I'll give you a hand," Marcella said, coming with me.

We were together in the master bathroom when she leaned into me and kissed me. "What was that for?"

She ignored me and checked my scalp, leaving me a clear view of her chest as she checked the dressing. I wanted to take her then, but she would have none of it. A few minutes later I emerged on deck in a pair of borrowed board shorts I had found in one of the cabins. Grabbing a screwdriver from the tool drawer, I opened the door cut into the transom used to haul big fish onto the deck and slid into the water. I was expecting a shock, but the water was the same temperature as the morning air, and I submerged myself, careful to keep my scalp above the water, to wash the grime from the last few days off.

I swam to the discharge port, thankful that the way we had anchored it was facing land and blocking the small wind waves coming from the open water. I jammed the screwdriver into the mangled opening, but the damage was bad. There would be no quick fix. Just as I was about to swim around the side to the transom, I heard an outboard engine coming toward us at high speed. Instinctively, I ducked back behind the boat.

The motor dropped an octave to an idle and I could hear men giving orders. The distinctive sound of a shotgun cocking told me all that I needed to know.

Chapter 23

"Both of you, get below." Chuy pointed the shotgun at the two sisters, thinking it would be nice to put matching bullets in them, but the one still had some value and he would have to wait. "If I see either of you before I come down there, one of you's gonna be shark bait." He held his aim until they were out of sight, then climbed the ladder to the bridge. Roberto was already at the controls. "Just head the fuck out'a here," he said, turning and scanning behind the boat for the man in the water.

He saw him and fired twice, but the boat was picking up speed and his aim was erratic. At least he'd scare the crap out of him. He smiled and fired one more round before turning back to Roberto. "What do we have left for fuel?" he asked.

Roberto checked the gauges. "A hundred miles if we're lucky. Depends on the currents and speed," he replied.

That didn't leave him many options. Looking over Roberto's shoulder, he studied the chart plotter. "That town," he said, pointing to a small village marked La Manzanilla.

"Only twenty miles. I don't see a marina, so probably no fuel," he said.

It wasn't the fuel that Chuy was thinking about. A plan to recoup his losses had come to him when he saw Marisa. All he needed was an Internet connection to start the gears in motion. "If there is an anchorage that we can get to the beach, that's good."

"*Si*, the bay is well protected. We can anchor there and have one of the fishing boats come out for you."

The last thing he wanted was another ride in one of the local boats, but necessity overcame his aversion. The million he could have gained was not forgotten, but now he had to worry about raising the quarter million he had bet, and he only had twenty-four hours to pay the bookies. He thought of the TV show *24*, and the loud ticking sound started in his head. "That's fine. I'm going below."

He climbed down to the main deck and stood by the port gunwale, looking at the town in the distance. Roberto was right, it was small, but if it had Wi–Fi, it was all he needed. Moving to the salon door, he opened it and moved inside. The sisters were huddled together on the couch.

"Your boyfriend screwed me," he said to Marisa. "Now I'm gonna get my revenge." He watched them from the corner of his eye, enjoying the feeling of power.

"What about Will?" Marcella asked.

Now this was interesting. Had the forlorn sister fallen for the boat bum? "Last I saw him, he was swimming to shore. There was no blood in the water, if that makes you feel better, though it just pisses me off." He moved to the bar and poured himself an inch of rum into a cut glass tumbler. He could tell they were anxious and sat across from them with his drink on the end table. Trimming the end off a fresh cigar, he took his time, thinking that the new plan might end up being better than the old one.

"My boyfriend will come for us," Marisa said.

"Exactly," Chuy said, taking a sip of the rum and making a production of lighting the cigar. "I'm counting on it. In fact, why don't we record a message for him that I can pass on. Let him know you're all right, blah blah blah."

"I will not do anything to help you," she said defiantly.

Marcella whispered something in her ear, and she sat back

with her arms crossed.

"Maybe you want to reconsider," he said, blowing smoke in their direction. He took his phone from his pocket and checked again for a signal. No luck. He would have to wait to get closer to town and hook up to Wi–Fi. Scrolling through the screens, he found the voice recorder and held it out to her. "Just say hi. Whatever you want, as long as he knows you are all right."

She took the phone. "What are you going to do?" she asked.

"Just see if he loves you as much as you think," Chuy said, enjoying the sparring. He felt the boat slow and looked out the window. They were running parallel to a long stretch of beach. Ahead he could see the town.

She looked at the phone, pressed a button, and started speaking. "Gerardo, my love. This gangster is holding me and says that I should tell you I am all right. I am, but you must not do what he asks. He is an evil man." She pressed the stop button and handed the phone back with a scowl on her face. "You will pay for this."

"Whatever. You just make sure he pays and this will end well for you," Chuy said, taking another sip. It was more for effect than pleasure and he put the glass down, knowing he needed to keep his wits about him until this was over. He thought about the trouble the boat bum had caused and looked at Marcella, trying to think of an angle for revenge, but there was nothing there. Maybe she could be a sacrifice to show he meant business—that was all he could figure she was worth.

He set the glass by the bottle and went outside. The town was just ahead, and Roberto was cruising close to the beach. He yelled to the fishermen on shore that there was a gringo aboard who would pay for a ride to the beach and saw several men rise to the bait. Soon a boat was launched. Roberto moved the sportfisher away from the beach, out of range of where he expected the waves would break at low tide, and dropped anchor. The boat swung around and he backed down, setting the hook deep in the sand.

A small boat moved toward the stern and tossed Roberto a line. The swell lifted the boats, banging them together. "This is as good as it's going to get," Roberto said to Chuy as he maneuvered the boats together. Chuy went into the cabin, grabbed his laptop and handed it to Roberto. Looking across at the fishing boat rocking alongside, he reached into his pocket and gave him his cell phone. "Hand them over when I'm aboard," he said and opened the transom door.

The man at the helm of the fishing boat smiled at him, showing a wide gap in his mouth. He nodded his head and timed the next swell perfectly, setting the wooden boat against the fiberglass hull. Chuy stepped across and extended his hand to Roberto, who passed across the laptop and phone. "No crap from those girls," Chuy said, moving to the middle of the boat. He hunched over the electronics to protect them from the bumpy ride to shore.

The fisherman idled a hundred yards from shore, looking back to sea like a surfer. Several large waves lifted the boat, but he was patient. Once the last was past, he gunned the engine and coasted on the whitewater trail, landing on the beach like a longboard surfer. The other men were waiting, and together they hauled the boat above the tide line before the next large wave crashed.

Chuy looked up, relieved to be on land, and reached into his pocket. He pulled out a twenty-dollar bill and handed it to the fisherman, who beamed back at him. Nodding at him, he put his laptop under his arm and start walking up the beach toward town. He reached the street running along the beach. Seeing nothing but some cantinas set up under large tents with plastic tables and chairs, he looked straight ahead. He saw several restaurants and continued straight on what looked like the main road. Looking around, he saw a bright red jeep approaching. The hair of the man behind the wheel was the first thing he noticed, it's color and his complexion almost matching the paint color. With his free hand he waved to the man, who honked a horn mounted to the side of the door and pulled up next to him.

"Yo yo. New in town?" the man asked.

"You could say that. Anywhere around here got Wi–Fi?" Chuy asked.

"Baby, you come to the right place. Palapa Joe's is the spot." The man pointed to the right. "Name's Rusty. Anything you need, they all know me." He grinned and honked the horn again.

"Appreciate it," Chuy said, and started walking toward the restaurant. Just as he reached the doorway his phone rang. Frank's name showed on the display and he let it ring several times while he opened the door, allowing the air conditioning to cool his body.

"Yeah," he answered, moving toward the bar and taking a seat near the end.

"I got that dude from the boat," he said.

Chuy smiled. Things were finally moving in the right direction. "Where are you?" he asked. Frank answered and Chuy gave him the name of the restaurant. He opened the laptop and waited for the Wi–Fi to connect. The icon appeared at the top of his screen and he went immediately to his email account. There were several inquiries, pleasant for now, from the bookies he now owed large sums to, asking when they could meet. Chuy ignored them and found Gerardo's email. He sat staring at the screen wondering how much he could get out of him. Surely, after his performance last night, his stock had risen even higher.

Remembering the phrase his father had beaten into his head: You can't win if you don't enter, he started typing. He got to the part where he needed to enter a number and sat back for a second. The bartender came over, and he ordered a shot of their best rum. He relit his cigar and entered seven figures, then paused. Draining his glass, he slid it across the bar, catching the bartender's eye. He approached and asked if he wanted a refill. "Sure," Chuy answered.

A minute later the bartender returned with the bottle and poured a healthy shot in the glass, then slid it back to Chuy. "Suppose you wanted to meet someone in an out-of-the-way kind of place around here that a stranger could find?" he asked.

"That's easy. Check out the nature trail across the lagoon. Just don't feed the crocs," the man said. He laughed and moved to a couple who had just entered.

Chuy was not sure if the man was kidding about the crocodiles or not. But he typed in: *tomorrow at sunset on the nature trail in La Manzanilla* and downloaded the recording from his phone as an attachment, then hit send. The boat bum was a bonus. If he had feelings for Marcella, like she had for him, he would be the perfect go-between. If things didn't work out, he would take the fall. There was always the black market for the women. They were a little older than premium but would get him enough to pay his debts.

Chapter 24

The roar of the fishing boat interrupted the bits of conversation that I heard aboard as it moved away. Then things went from bad to worse when the *Dorado's* engines started and I heard the windlass bring the anchor up. At first I thought that the women had lied about me, and I might be safe. That changed quickly when I heard the shotgun chamber a round, followed by a loud blast and a shower of pellets that landed in front of me. I risked a look back and saw Chuy braced against the transom, ready to fire again. With everything I had left, I swam for the beach.

Several more shots fired, all short, and finally my feet hit the bottom. I ran out onto the beach, putting as much distance between the shotgun and me as possible. We both reached the same conclusion at the same time and I heard the boat accelerate and move into open water. Even though my brain knew I was safe, I ran to the closest palapa and used one of the skinned logs supporting the thatched roof for cover.

The *Dorado* was moving out fast. I stood there watching until the only sign of the boat was a large white wake, and soon even that faded away. I sat at the wooden picnic table underneath the shelter, staring out to sea. My body screamed in pain. To make matters worse, my sole possessions were a pair of faded board shorts and the screwdriver I still held in my hand. I started thinking the best option would be to walk to town and beg someone to let me make a call or send an email to Salvage Solutions, then wait for them to wire some money to get me out of this mess.

With my head pounding, I started walking toward the road, wondering what had happened here. I passed a run-down, abandoned-looking hotel and several concrete slabs where buildings had previously stood. It was like a ghost town. The pristine bay and a protected anchorage should have been teaming with tourists and cruisers.

Two armed guards came running around the side of the hotel, and I got my first hint why it was abandoned. I was about to raise my hands and surrender when they ran by me to the tide line and stared at the two sailboats anchored in the harbor, then down the empty beach.

Satisfied that the threat was gone, they walked casually back to the road. I quickly reviewed my one option and followed, hoping there would be some means of communication I could use wherever they were headed. The hot asphalt burned my feet, forcing me to stay in the shade, making my plight even more difficult. Finally, I reached the main road and saw a small guardhouse surrounded by barbed wire and a chain-link fence. Set right in the middle of the road, it blocked the entrance to the property.

I had enough experience in banana republics to know that you never really knew what was going on, but with little choice, I made my way to the guardhouse. The two men I had followed were sitting to the side under the shade of an umbrella, and two more men sat in chairs staring at the empty road.

"*Buenos dias*," I said loudly as I approached, wanting the rifles leaning against the wall of the guard shack to remain there. The men turned and looked at me, quickly exchanging a quick joke at my expense.

I decided to try English. "Can you tell me where I can find a phone?"

They looked at each other and laughed again. Apparently I was the high point of their day. "Carlos," one called out. A minute later one of the guards from the beach came toward me.

"*Señor*, you are in need of something?" he asked.

"I was thrown off a boat and need help," I said, deciding to stay as close to the truth as I could. "Maybe a telephone?"

"This is a restricted area," he said, trying to keep a straight face.

That part was obvious. "I will leave as soon as possible. I just need some help," I pleaded.

"You have no papers or ID?" he asked.

That again was obvious, and I stood there, feeling like an idiot, trying to find some angle that might influence him. Our standoff was interrupted by the sound of a car approaching. The two guards immediately got to their feet, grabbed their rifles, and assumed their positions at the gate. The car approached quickly, apparently not aware of the roadblock. It braked and came to a stop inches before the gate. The two guards stood unmoved. "Please turn off the engine," one man called out in Spanish.

The driver leaned his head out of the open window with a look on his face that said he rarely listened to authority. It remained there until the other man leveled the barrel of his rifle at him. It was Chuy's man. He must have gotten the message and turned off the engine and sat with both hands on the steering wheel. The other guard raised his rifle and approached the stopped car. A minute later Chuy's bodyguard was ordered out of the car and spread-eagled on the pavement.

This was my chance, but I had no idea how to play it. I watched as one of the guards searched him, while the other went through the car. He came back with a paper in his hand. "You are not Rafael Fernandez," he said, waving what I assumed was the vehicle registration at the bodyguard.

I turned to Carlos, who had remained by my side. "What are

they going to do to him?"

"They are just scaring him. We are not the *policia*, or a gang. Just security to keep undesirables out of the property."

Apparently the bodyguard was an undesirable, and I had an idea. "Let me talk to him. Maybe he can solve my problem."

Carlos walked forward and talked to the closest guard. He returned a minute later. "Go ahead. Both of you should get off the property."

I hopped across the broiling asphalt, trying not to look too stupid, and approached the man. "I am the man Chuy wants. I'd rather face him than these crazy cartel men," I said. Let him think the worst and that this was some kind of cartel operation and he was in danger.

"You're the dude from the boat?" he asked.

I realized he might not have seen me before. "Chuy just took the boat and the girls. Now let's get out of here," I pleaded as if both our lives depended on it, relieved when he nodded.

"We are going to leave now," I said, holding my hands above my head and moving toward the passenger door. The guards stood unmoving, not sure of what was going on. I opened the door and got in. "Come on," I called to the bodyguard.

Carlos said something to the guard holding the rifle on the driver, who nodded and motioned for him to get in. The bodyguard jumped into the driver's seat and within seconds had started the car and executed a quick three-point turn. We sped away from the blockade. I heard a shot and looked back, wondering if Carlos had been on the level, and saw the three men huddled together, laughing at us.

The bodyguard was driving faster than the pot-holed road would allow. I bounced, hitting the ceiling several times, and felt the first trickle of blood flowing from my wound. Finally, he felt we were comfortably out of range and slowed.

"Name's Frank," he said, his trained eyes quickly scanning

me for any threat. "Thanks for that."

"No problem. I'm Will. If you could drop me at the next town, we can call it even," I said, hoping for the best.

"Next town will be where the boss is. Maybe he wants to see you, maybe he don't. That's not for me to decide," he said, picking the phone up from the console and dialing. He spoke briefly. "I guess we'll see what to do with you soon enough," he said.

We turned right, heading south. With every passing mile, my apprehension increased, as did our speed as the road conditions improved. Hotels and condominiums now lined the ocean side of the road, with houses set up the hill toward the interior. We passed a road with a crooked sign indicating it led to Route 200 and suddenly we were back on a dirt road.

"Shouldn't we have turned there?" I asked.

He ignored me and continued, trying to speed up enough for the car to float over the washboard road rather than hit every bump. We passed several campgrounds, crossed a bridge that had danger signs, a rarity in Mexico, with rough drawings of alligators. In a few blocks, we found ourselves in a small town. The water was visible from the road, and I assumed it was the southern end of the same bay we had anchored in. Seamounts poked out of the water, and a small hill was terraced with colorful houses. The roads were wider and better maintained than I had expected, winding around the small hills that all ended at the beach.

Glancing at his phone, Frank turned several times and parked across from a restaurant. "No trouble from you," he said, and got out of the car. I followed him across the street and into the restaurant. It was clearly an expat place with a group of men huddled by the bar and several tables with couples and groups in the dining room. Wi–Fi and air conditioning were the specialties of the house, and everyone had a computer or tablet out.

In a cloud of cigar smoke, Chuy sat by himself at the bar, studying a laptop. He barely looked up when we approached. "You got a name, for all the trouble you caused me?"

"Will," I muttered.

"Okay, Will, so this is how it's going to go."

He turned to me and I shivered, maybe from the air conditioning on my mostly naked body, or maybe from his ice-cold stare. I stood speechless.

"You're going to do me a favor. If you succeed, we'll call it even, and I may even owe you a debt of gratitude," he said, and blew smoke at me. "The boyfriend of the girl. He should be here tomorrow. You are going to meet him and exchange the girl for a suitcase, which you will bring to me."

"That's it?" I asked. It seemed too simple.

"See, here's the rub. They're going to think you're me, and maybe, being Mexico and all, will put a bullet through your head. These people hold grudges here. They don't do business like civilized people," he said, returning his attention to the computer and his cigar.

"Come on," Frank said. "You'll be our guest until the exchange."

Chapter 25

Frank and I sat on plastic chairs under a makeshift tent at one of the handful of cantinas lining the beach, and waited for Chuy. The *Dorado* was anchored a couple of hundred yards offshore—too far away to see any activity aboard. While we waited, I thought about the predicament I had gotten myself into, wondering whether it was Marcella, my own greed, or a combination of both that had landed me here. Instead of sailing the *Nai'a* up the coast and taking a modest payday, I was entangled in a situation that I was not sure I could get out of, and I lamented on my decisions while we waited.

There was something about her that had my heart, something I couldn't control. Steering myself away from the melancholy that was enveloping me, I started to think of how I could salvage this mess. Force might have been an option, if I were armed and capable. Not being a retired Navy Seal with secret squirrel ninja skills kind of took that off the table. Chuy had the shotgun, and I could see a bulge under Frank's untucked shirt.

Something made me turn back to the boat. I was sure I saw two women standing on deck and felt a sea change come over me. My mood swung and I thought about the skills I did have. The engine discharge was still jury-rigged, and sabotage was something I could do, if I had the chance—it could be the only avenue for escape.

A handful of fishermen rose from the crates they were sitting on when Chuy approached the beach, all vying for his cash. He pointed to one of the men, who led us to his boat. A few minutes later, we were aboard the *Dorado*. His gold teeth gleamed when Chuy handed him a twenty and he motored back to shore.

Roberto was waiting and helped us aboard. He seemed agitated.

"What's with you?" Chuy asked. "Where are the women?"

"They are below, locked in the stateroom," he said.

"Well, what is it then?"

"The water discharge for the engine is damaged." He pointed to the hose.

"Well, fix it then," Chuy said, looking at my temporary rig.

He didn't need to be a mechanic to see it needed a permanent repair.

"It is not so easy. We need parts," he said.

Chuy glared at me, like it was my fault. "And where do you get parts in this third-world hellhole? I don't guess there's a West Marine on the corner."

"Manzanillo is an hour by car down the coast. They will have it," he said.

"Give Frank a list of what you need. He can take the car down in the morning," Chuy said, and looked back at me. "Lock him up somewhere."

Frank took my arm and led me through the salon and down the stairs. He pushed me into the engine room and tried to close the door. The hose I had rigged was in the way. Without a second thought, he took a knife from his pocket, opened the blade and cut the hose, tossing the end back in the room. The door slammed shut. I looked and saw there was no lock, but a minute later I heard the rattle of a chain and the click of a padlock.

Alone now, I looked around the room. The sight of my own blood dried on the wall brought my attention back to the present. I looked at my repair job and noticed the screwdriver off to the side. With the tool in hand, I studied the engine, trying to figure out what I could do to get us out of there. Knowing Frank would be gone for at least several hours in the morning helped. Whatever I came up with would have a better chance for success with him gone.

The room was crowded with equipment. Off to the side by the door was a small clear space of floor. I sat down to wait. Chuy had not told me his timeline for the exchange, but I had to assume that since it was already late afternoon, that tonight would be too soon. With Frank gone in the morning, I guessed the exchange would take place tomorrow evening. Before then, I would have to devise and execute a plan to take the boat.

The cut hose on the floor gave me an idea. I rose and stared at the engine, hoping there was a remote starter. If I could start the engine from here, I could flood the compartment. There would be an alarm, and I guessed Chuy would send Roberto to see what was wrong. I thought I could take him, especially if I had the element of surprise. If I got that far, I would figure out how to deal with Chuy. I settled back down to wait, and my thoughts turned to Marcella.

Suddenly there was a loud click and I heard the sound of a flywheel spin. Seconds later a loud roar encompassed the room as the generator started. A compressor kicked in, and I felt a welcome draft of cool air on my back.

I turned around to see where it was coming from and saw the network of small ducts running over my head feeding air conditioning to the cabins. Envisioning the layout of the boat, I traced the lines, guessing which cabin each one connected to and had an idea. If I knew which cabin the women were being kept in, I could communicate through the ducts. Two lines ran forward, feeding Chuy's stateroom. Another two were just overhead. The starboard line would go to the larger berth, where Frank was camped out, and the port line fed the captain's cabin. Another larger line ran toward the stern that would service the salon.

It made sense that the women were being kept in Frank's cabin. Chuy would not give up his, and the port-side cabin was too small. I was about to make my move when the compressor cycled off and the generator shut down, leaving the room silent. Moving to the starboard side duct, I stood stooped over and examined the fitting. I waited a few minutes, listening for any sounds that might confirm my theory. There was nothing but the rhythmic lapping of waves against the hull. Using the screwdriver, I pried around the fitting. The duct came off and I held my breath.

The hushed voices of women talking came through the opening and I relaxed.

"Hey," I whispered into the opening and heard footsteps above. "Over here."

"Will?"

Something moved over the vent, blocking the light from the cabin. "It's me. Down here in the engine room."

"Are you all right?" It was Marcella.

"Yeah. I'm locked in here, but I've got a plan."

I steeled myself for her rebuff after the failure of my last plans.

"Thank you for coming for us," she said instead.

After I explained what I had in mind, we talked late into the night like high school lovers, fearing we would never see each other again and not wanting to say goodbye.

* * *

I regretted not wearing a watch when I woke covered in sweat. With no windows in the compartment, it was impossible to tell the time of day. The room had no exhaust or ventilation unless the engine was running, and it felt like every breath that I took would suck the last drop of oxygen from the room. I rubbed my eyes, feeling the rawness and grit from lack of sleep and guessed it was still before dawn. No matter what time it was outside, the equipment was well lit by several strips of fluorescent tubes mounted to the ceiling, making it easy to see what I needed to do. Surveying the machinery, I found the starter for the port engine and checked for a remote button. An engine this size should have one, allowing a mechanic to start the engine without going back and forth to the bridge. A minute later, I found it.

Now I had to wait until Frank left to retrieve the parts before I could take action. I went back to the duct and pried loose the fitting.

"Marcella," I whispered. There was silence and I tried again, hearing someone move now. "What time is it?"

"I don't know," she said.

"Is it light out?" I asked.

"*Si.* Just barely," came the answer.

Suddenly I could hear their door open. I shoved the duct back and ran to turn off the light. Stumbling in the dark room, I made my way back to the vent and tried to hear the conversation, but it was muted by the insulation surrounding the vent. A minute later, I heard someone outside the engine room door and moved against the wall, feigning sleep. The door opened and the light came on. I rubbed my eyes.

Roberto entered with a tray of food and a bottle of water. He gave me a look that I couldn't quite place and set down the tray as if I were a caged animal and he needed to keep his distance. He waited until I retrieved the food. I had the feeling he wanted to say something, but he just stared at me while I ate. The food was good and I ate greedily, not realizing how hungry I had been until it was gone. Handing the bowl and silverware back to him, he took them and left.

I tried to relax and wait for some sign that Frank was gone. It

150

must be light by now, I thought, trying to guess how much time had elapsed since I had spoken to Marcella. My feeble attempt to meditate did nothing for my anxiety, instead, it made me more aware of my circumstances. The walls were closing in on me now and I was covered in sweat. Without warning, the generator kicked in and I felt a blast of air when the ventilation started to pull the stale air from the room. Frank or not, it was time.

Moving back to the discharge hose, I tried to pull off the hose I had installed, but it resisted my efforts. I stood back, looking around the room for something to loosen the hose clamp. I went for the toolbox and removed the wrench. I was surprised at how tight the nut was. At first it wouldn't turn, and I realized the power of adrenaline. Finally, I got it to budge, and with a few more turns it was loose and I slid the clamp back and removed the hose from the barbed fitting.

When I started the engine, the water would flow into the compartment. I tried not to think about being stuck in a watertight room with the hot discharge water pouring in as I moved to the remote starter and hit the button. The flywheel spun and caught, releasing a blast of water into the room. I breathed deeply, trying to quell my anxiety as the water started to heat up and pool around my feet. I needed to be patient and breathed again. It would take a few minutes for the men on deck to realize what had happened as the water crept up my calves toward my knees. I felt the temperature increase as the engine warmed. The water started scalding my thighs and I grabbed the pipe above the door. My muscles strained to hold my weight off the floor as the water rose below me, and still there was no sign of activity.

Just as I was about to release the pipe, a loud buzzer sounded. Finally, the alarm had been triggered. I could only hope someone above was astute enough to get down here quickly.

Chapter 26

Every muscle in my arms twitched and burned as I grasped the pipe. Over the flow of water, I heard voices outside the door and saw the interior handle move. The door cracked and opened slightly. Water rushed out and I heard a voice yell, then the door closed again. The sound of the discharge was quiet, now that the water level had risen above the valve, but it was dangerously close to some of the electrical components. I heard Chuy ordering Roberto to open the door and saw it crack again.

Instead of entering the room, where I could swing toward him, he grasped the top of the door and lifted his body off the deck, allowing the water to rush past him. From where I was I couldn't see him, but knew we were both watching the water level. Suddenly it was quiet and I realized that Chuy must have shut down the engine from the bridge. Only the sound of blood pumping in my ears and the whine of the bilge pumps remained.

My grip was failing and I dropped to the deck, finding myself face–to–face with Roberto. We were both unarmed. I went into a fighting stance and prepared to attack when I heard the shotgun chamber a round. Chuy pushed Roberto aside with the barrel and faced me.

"Get the women," he ordered Roberto and turned to me with a snarl on his face.

An artery pulsed, standing proud on his forehead, signaling

me that he was not open for reason. He was about to say something when Roberto appeared, pushing the two women in front of him.

"The one he likes. Tie her up to the engine." He turned to me. "See if you cause any more trouble."

Chuy motioned for the women to move toward the opposite corner of the room. I averted my gaze from her pleading look. Roberto was back with a dock line. He slid the end around a gap in the manifold and pulled it through the loop braided into the line, then secured Marcella's hands behind her back.

"Let's go," Chuy said. "Lock them in separate cabins and sit in the hall between them." He moved past Roberto.

"You heard him," Roberto said without conviction.

I seized the moment, remembering the feeling I had gotten that he wanted to talk yesterday. "What was it you wanted to say yesterday?" He looked at me without answering, grabbing my arm and pulling me forward. It wasn't a hard grip, and I probably could have broken free, but my instincts were screaming at me to wait—that there was something here. I looked back at Marcella. "Don't worry," was all I could say, and dodged the desperate look on her face.

He pushed me forward, whispering, "You will help me, and I will help you."

Just as I was about to ask him what he meant, Frank walked up to us.

"Here's the part. I'll deal with them while you install it. Make sure it works. The boss wants to be out of here after the exchange." He handed Roberto a box.

I had lost my chance. Frank pushed Marisa in front and together we climbed the short flight of steps to the main deck. I was hoping for a cabin, where I might find a weapon, but instead he pushed me into the head and locked the door. I assumed Marisa was back in the same cabin as before. She was not my primary concern, though. There was a payday attached to her safety. It was

Marcella that I was worried about.

It was cramped inside the head and I sat on the only seat available. Cigar smoke drifted in through the small hatch, cutting off the light breeze that had been blowing fresh air in. I was about to close it when I heard Chuy's voice. The wind carried more than the smoke. I caught enough of the conversation to know it was about the exchange tonight. It sounded like it was still on. This bit of information gave me at least a few hours to figure a way out of there.

The conversation ended and I waited. Several times the engine had started and stopped. The last time it had run for quite a while, a sign that it was repaired. The minutes dragged into hours until finally I heard activity outside the door.

"*Amigo*. It's time," Roberto called out. "We take the *señorita* and go ashore."

The door opened and he stood there with Marisa in front of him. I stepped forward, not seeing Frank come behind me. He pulled up on my arm and escorted me to the deck. Roberto hailed one of the fishermen, and we were soon heading toward the beach. Frank sat across from me with the old revolver in one hand as we bounced through the waves. It was hard to read Marisa. She had to be happy she was about to be freed, but, at the same time, I knew she was worried about her sister.

As if reading my mind, she spoke to Frank over the small motor, "Where is Chuy? I want him to guarantee my sister's safety before I go through with this."

"What are you going to do? Risk both your lives? Believe me, the boss don't want that woman around. He'll be happy to give her back, once this bit of business is done," he said.

We were through the breaking waves and the fisherman slid the boat onto the beach. The last wave had been a big one, taking us to the high-tide line. We stepped onto the sand. Frank pulled his phone out and started typing on the keyboard. I assumed he was getting instructions from Chuy, because a second later, it dinged and, after reading the message, he motioned us toward the street.

We crossed the street to take advantage of the little bit of shade available and turned left. A few blocks later we found ourselves at the creek. Several groups of tourists were on a narrow boardwalk pointing and screaming at something in the water. They turned with their backs to the rail and took a selfie before moving back to the street. Frank nosed us forward and I saw what they had been so excited about.

At first it looked like logs floating in the water—until one moved, leaving a wake behind it. Two more humps also disappeared, leaving wakes behind them as well. All of a sudden, the water boiled and I saw several narrow snouts emerge from the muddy lagoon. Frank nudged us past the boardwalk and pulled the phone from his pocket.

"Gerardo will be here in a few," he said, moving us toward a clump of small bushes on the beach side of the walkway. "When he gets here, we let him go onto the boardwalk and then follow."

I got the logic immediately. If things didn't go right, Gerardo would have no way to get past Frank. Mosquitos buzzed around us as the fading sunlight reflected off the water to our left. I felt Marisa stir beside me and followed her gaze to the street. A single man walked toward us with a messenger bag slung over one shoulder. His body language and the arm held protectively over the bag told me it was Gerardo. He crossed the street and Frank pushed us back, giving Marisa a forceful look to be quiet.

The man approached and looked around. He saw the entrance to the boardwalk and moved toward it. Another glance around and he stepped onto the green painted wood decking and was out of sight. Frank waited about thirty seconds before pushing us ahead onto the path. It was twilight now and I moved as slowly as he would allow. The darker it got, the better chance I had of doing something, although, up to this point, I hadn't figured out what that was going to be. He stayed where he was and I looked back at him.

"Go on, and don't screw it up," he said.

The boardwalk was a perfect setup for an ambush. The single three-foot-wide walkway with chain-link fencing and a wood rail on top on both sides jutted out into the crocodile-infested creek. One end had the crocodiles—the other Frank.

We were well out of sight of the street. Clouds of bugs swarmed us as we continued on into the shadows. I started swatting at the mosquitos buzzing around my head, getting impatient.

"Where are you?" I called out.

We continued around another bend and started toward the end of the boardwalk. There was no sign of Gerardo, and I remembered what Chuy had said about using me. With dread, I continued slowly forward and stopped when a man appeared around the bend. Even from fifty feet away, I could see his face light up when he saw Marisa, but at the same time, thinking I was Chuy, he realized he was trapped. He reached into the bag and I saw the glint of wrapped bills.

"Here. Take the money. Just don't hurt her," he called out.

Marisa looked at me and I let her go to him. They embraced, but his eyes remained on me. I was about to tell him everything was going to be all right when I smelled the faintest hint of cigar smoke and realized we were all in trouble.

Chapter 27

"They in there?" Chuy asked as he swatted the cloud of mosquitos swarming around his head.

"Yeah," Frank answered.

"Anyone else?" Chuy asked.

"Not as far as I could tell," Frank said. "What are we going to do with them after the exchange?"

Chuy reached into a bag by his side and held up a package of chicken parts. "The local butcher was very accommodating." He reached into the bag, pulled out a piece, and tossed it into the water. Seconds later the lagoon churned as the crocodiles fought over the food. Another few seconds and the water was still again.

"Nice, boss."

"You keep an eye out in case wonder boy brought any company along. I'll take care of things in there," Chuy said. He looked back toward town, checking to make sure there was no one interested. The streets were deserted. He rose and entered the boardwalk. Quickly he traced his steps from earlier that afternoon, when he had taken a quick walk to get a feel for it, and took a right onto a small side dock. He could see two figures across the dark water, indistinguishable in the low light. Not that it mattered who was who—they were all going to the same place. The shrieks of birds and other creatures he didn't want to know about made it impossible to hear the conversation.

The bugs were fiercer in here, and he pulled his lighter out, turned away from the other dock, and lit the stub of cigar planted between his teeth. Maybe that would keep the little bastards away, he thought, as he let the smoke waft around him. It seemed to help and he turned back to the dock. A single figure appeared moving toward them. He smiled when he saw the bag slung from his shoulder.

The girl ran to the newcomer and he watched them embrace. Then the man handed a messenger bag to Will. It was time to act, and he moved quickly toward the intersection of the docks, where he waited for his payday. He could hear them coming toward him before he saw them and stepped into the center of the boardwalk, bag of chicken in one hand, and the rusty revolver in the other.

"I'll take that," he said as they approached, and he watched the look on their faces change instantly. "Now, pass the bag over and turn around."

* * *

I stared at the weapon and glanced up at the man behind it. Behind the cloud of smoke was Chuy. Looking to the left and right, I knew he had us trapped. I removed the bag from my shoulder and handed it to him. There was nothing to do except follow along and hope he made a mistake.

"Move," he ordered, walking toward us. He held the bag by the handles in one hand and the gun in the other.

We walked toward the end of the boardwalk. "Seems pretty light to me," I said, trying to plant a seed of doubt.

He looked down at the bag. "What the hell do you know?"

"A million dollars weighs more than that," I said, not knowing what I was talking about. It just seemed like it should.

He hefted the bag as if guessing its weight, then came within a few feet of us and knelt down. This had to be it. Slowly, with one

158

eye on us and the other on the bag, he set the gun on the deck and opened the clasp. He was focused on the cash, and I took a step forward. Instantly he grabbed the gun and fired a quick shot. I felt the bullet buzz by my arm and waited for the next one to hit me.

"Just stay the fuck where you are," he said, turning to Gerardo. "He's right. Ain't no way there's a million in here." He swung the gun to Gerardo. Marisa jumped in front of him just as he pulled the trigger. The click was louder than it should have been.

I made my move while Chuy fumbled with the cylinder. It was stuck, and he slammed the gun against the deck, trying to dislodge the mechanism. Gerardo was right behind me. Just as we reached him, another shot fired. Gerardo was already in the air when I heard the blast. With a move done a thousand times in practice, he fell backward as if defying gravity and kicked the gun, taking it and the bag of chicken parts into the black water.

"Nobody move!" Frank yelled.

"Don't shoot the Mexican. Damned bastard shorted me. Shoot the other two," Chuy said, rising from the deck with the bag clutched under his arm.

Suddenly the water below us erupted. Chuy brushed past Frank, heading for the safety of dry land. The bodyguard was off balance now and I went for him, trying to at least dislodge the weapon from his hand. My shoulder cracked into his ribs and we fell together into the railing. Whether it was poorly attached or our combined weight had dislodged the fasteners, the chain-link parted where it should have connected to the deck. Frank went first, and I felt his hands gripping my leg tightly. I clawed for the metal fence, grabbing onto the small openings several feet above, and started to pull myself over the rail when I felt a tug on my legs.

Frank had a hold of both my legs and was trying to pull me back when all of a sudden his grip failed. The water seemed to rise toward me, and I could smell the prehistoric breath of the beast as it opened its mouth and took Frank's leg into its grip. He was no match for the croc, who pulled him into the water, rolling him over and over to drown him. We stared down at the water boiling beneath us and smelled the copper odor of blood. Marisa turned away first and Gerardo quickly went to her. Although it was too dark to see anything, I couldn't tear my eyes away from the carnage until the water settled.

Finally I recovered. "Marcella!"

They both looked at me.

"Chuy is going back to the boat."

They spoke quickly in Spanish. "Gerardo must not get involved in this," Marisa said.

I had already decided that they were done. "You two get somewhere safe. Let the authorities know that Chuy has her."

"I will do whatever you need," Marisa said.

* * *

I left them in each other's arms and ran to the beach. Just offshore I could see the *Dorado*, still anchored and bobbing in the waves. For a second I was relieved until I saw the phosphorescence caused by the wake of a small boat pushing through the surf and heading in her direction. It was too far away to see who was aboard, but I knew it was Chuy with his bag of cash. The light from a small bonfire became visible as I ran down the beach to the small group of fishermen huddled around it.

I gasped, out of breath and bent over with my hands on my knees, looking out to the water. One of the fishermen came toward me, but I waved him away. A boat would be seen. I would have to swim.

Breathing deeply, I walked into the surf, ignoring the waves as they crashed around me. A large one threatened to break and I dove into it, surfacing on its calm backside, and I started swimming toward the *Dorado* before the next wave threw me back on the beach. Somehow I made it through the breakers and found the water was much rougher now. I struggled to look ahead to the *Dorado* as I stroked. A blast of light temporarily blinded me when the LED floodlights were turned on, bringing her from near darkness to brilliant light. A billow of smoke was backlit by the lights as the engine started. Blood started pounding in my ears when I heard the windlass strain to free the anchor.

I was close and clawed at the water trying to reach the transom. I could see the boat clearly and started to plan my approach as I pulled closer. Roberto was the only figure visible on the bridge. Chuy and Marcella must be below.

Roberto would be looking forward as he set his course. This would be my only chance. I reached for a fitting on the transom and pulled myself toward the hull. With a burst of energy I didn't know I had, I set my feet against the fiberglass hull and pulled myself over into the cockpit. I was exposed now, and rolled toward the gunwale into a blind spot, invisible, I hoped, to anyone watching from the bridge. Inching along the gunwale, I moved toward the salon door and looked inside. Chuy was on the settee, piles of hundred dollar bills scattered around him.

Crawling forward, I kept my body tight against the cabin and moved quietly toward the bow. I passed the windows to the salon and found the hatch to Marcella's cabin. The fiberglass cover was open, allowing for ventilation, but was not near big enough for a body to pass through.

"Hey," I whispered into the dark cabin. I was greeted by silence and wondered if he had already killed her. I called out again, a little louder this time, but there was still no answer. Worried I was too late, I moved to the foredeck and sat against the bulkhead trying to figure out my next move.

Chapter 28

Spray flew around me as the boat picked up speed and crashed into the waves. The deck became slippery, and the few minutes of refuge I had found were over. Turning, I looked back at the bridge and saw only Roberto through the glare of the lights. Chuy must still be in the cabin, but where was Marcella?

Moving back on the port side, I checked the head and Frank's cabin. The lights were off and the hatch was closed. If she was still on board, there were only two other places. Chuy's stateroom was forward and not accessible from the foredeck. The engine room was the likely place and suddenly a piercing alarm confirmed it.

The boat slowed and I heard the door open and Chuy yell something up to the bridge. Working my way toward the stern, I watched Roberto climb down from the flybridge and enter the salon. The boat had slowed, and I was pretty sure what had caused the alarm. Marcella must have detached the hose.

I thought about going to the bridge, changing the course, and creating more havoc, but decided against it, choosing surprise as my weapon. I looked into the salon. It was empty except for the stacks of bills spread all over the floor. Looking around for a weapon, I grabbed a club used to knock out fish from a holder under the gunwale and entered the room.

The alarm made it impossible to hear what was going on

below, and blindly I moved to the stairs leading to the engine room. One step at a time, I descended and looked into the compartment. Roberto was bent over the pipes, working furiously to reattach the hose. Across from me the muscles on Chuy's forearm stood proud as he choked Marcella.

From the color of her face, I had no time to waste. Swinging the steel club at his head, I went right for him. He saw me at the last minute and dropped Marcella. Dodging the weapon, he caught me in the side with a blow from what I guessed was the butt of the shotgun that must have been in his other hand. Pain shot through me, bringing stars to my eyes. The brief pause gave him time to raise the barrel. It was aimed at my chest.

"You again?" he exclaimed.

I didn't answer, choosing to conserve my energy. I doubted he would shoot me in here. The chance of a ricochet or damage to the engine was too great. I called his bluff and approached with the club. From the corner of my eye I saw Roberto pull Marcella out of the room.

Chuy swung the shotgun around like a gunfighter in an old western, gripping it with the barrel. We stood there facing each other, both drenched in water from the discharge. He swung first, causing me to back away. The reach of the gun was almost twice that of the club, leaving me at a disadvantage. I worked my way around the starboard engine, staying just out of reach as he swung again. Testing him, I jabbed the bat in his direction, causing him to back up a step, and I thought I saw an opening.

Again I jabbed, and then swung. He was obviously less of a fighter than I expected, used to paying for his muscle, and I could see the panic in his eyes as he stepped backward. Swinging across my body this time, I forced him back toward the water spraying from the valve on the port engine. He must have seen where I was going and, in desperation, spun the gun in his hands and thrust the barrel toward my chest. We were close enough that there was little risk of him missing me, and in slow motion I saw his finger tighten on the trigger and a smug look take over his face. He knew he had won.

I backed away, but there was nowhere to go. He had me against the bulkhead, the barrel pushing against my ribs. Instinctively I went to raise my hands in surrender, hoping that he wouldn't shoot, and my hand brushed against the fire extinguisher mounted on the wall. Without looking, my fingers found the latch and I removed it from the holder. Taking a quick swing up, I knocked the barrel to the ceiling, but the impact dislodged the cylinder from my hand. The gun fired, blasting pellets into the fiberglass ceiling. Between the deafening sound and the recoil from the gun, Chuy was momentarily disoriented. I wasn't much better, but saw the flow of water jetting from the pipe behind him and pushed him toward it. The gun discharged again, this time spraying the steel engine block. My skin stung as pellets ricocheted against me.

The recoil forced him backward again, and the barrel leveled at my chest. Before he could recover and fire again, I jumped on him, pushing the weapon to the side. Releasing the pin from the fire extinguisher, I pulled the trigger. The force of the foam slammed his head against the discharge pipe and held it there. With everything I had, I pushed him. Finally realizing there was no resistance, I dropped his body and backed away, fighting down the bloodlust that had overtaken me. Not sure whether he had suffocated or the trauma to his head had killed him, I reached over to check his pulse and found none.

I recovered enough to move the body to the side and tighten the loose fitting. The water stopped spraying, leaving the room coated in the foamy residue from the extinguisher. I sank to the deck and sat against the engine, letting the world came back into focus. It took a minute to calm my breath. I was bruised but not injured. The ringing in my ears subsided and I saw Marcella in the doorway. I was about to reach out to her when I saw Roberto behind her.

I still had not figured the man out and looked around for the shotgun. It was across the room, out of reach. He stepped around Marcella and approached me with his hands out.

"*Bueno*," he said, extending a hand to me.

I breathed in relief and held my arm out. He hauled me from the floor and embraced me.

I broke down, slumping against him, and felt Marcella's hand on my shoulder. I took a last look at Chuy's inert body on the deck as they escorted me from the room. Roberto shut and locked the door and they helped me up the stairs to the salon.

I slumped against the armrest of the settee, jumping as Marcella scrubbed the small wounds from the shotgun pellets with peroxide. I stared at the piles of money on the floor. Once they had settled me, Roberto reattached the pipe and went to the bridge to check our course and make sure the engine temperature was in the normal range. We had decided to head back to Puerto Vallarta to refuel and retrieve the *Nai'a*. Only two people now stood in the way of my dream, and I couldn't gauge either of them.

"What's next for you?" I asked Marcella, trying to draw her out.

"I was going to ask you the same. I've taken to this boating thing," she smiled.

That was the answer I thought I wanted, but we still had some issues. "I'm going up to talk to Roberto," I said, escaping her next attempt to rid me of bacteria.

"I guess someone has to count all this," she said, moving to the floor. "We need to get it back to Gerardo."

I smiled. This was a good sign that things could work out between us.

She picked up her phone and texted something. Without waiting for the response, I left the salon and climbed up to the bridge. Roberto looked nervous behind the wheel.

"Everything in the normal range?" I asked to break the tension.

"*Si*, she is running good. We have enough fuel to make Puerto Vallarta, and the weather looks good," he said.

"Then I guess we need to figure out what to do with you," I said.

He looked at me like a wounded puppy. "I am just a boat captain. I can find work."

"I got the feeling that you didn't really want to work for Chuy," I said.

"He was a bad man, but a job is a job."

That was something I knew all too well. "Any interest in taking the boat back to the States?" I asked. It had already occurred to me that I needed a captain to help bring both boats back. Towing the sailboat two thousand miles would be cumbersome and possibly dangerous as well as expensive.

His eyes lit up. "*Señor*, it would be an honor to do that for you," he said proudly.

"No honor. Like you said—it's a job, and I'll pay you well for it."

He extended his hand and we shook on the deal. Not really needing to, I checked his course and headed back down to the cabin. Marcella had the money back in the bag.

"All there?" I asked.

"Right at a million. I've never seen so much cash," she said.

"Have you gotten an answer if they will meet us?" I asked.

"Not yet. Reception is pretty sketchy out here."

Watching her with all that money caused a tinge of doubt to spread over me. I wanted to check her phone and see if she really had tried to contact them, but somehow she sensed my mistrust, or maybe it was just a coincidence, and she pulled the phone close to her.

Chapter 29

That night, Roberto and I took shifts running the boat back to Puerto Vallarta. We ran at around twenty knots to conserve fuel. Our plan was to arrive at daybreak and pick up the *Nai'a*. We would refuel before making the crossing to Cabo. With Roberto at the helm, I went down to clean up the engine room and deal with Chuy's body.

As soon as we reached deep water, we weighted down the body with the empty fire extinguisher and a bag of fishing weights and dumped it overboard. Marcella ransacked his cabin, removing everything that carried his scent and threw it into the dark water. A trail of expensive shoes and clothes soon floated in our wake. By morning I expected the current would take him and his belongings far away from us.

On my watch, I tried to formulate a plan to get the money back to Gerardo and the boats back to the States. We could meet him in Cabo, where I planned to refuel before heading out into the Pacific. That was the easy problem. The boats were more complicated.

I had reservations about taking both together. I would have to sail the *Nai'a*. I knew Roberto could handle the *Dorado*, but the boats were not built to cruise together. I didn't know or trust Roberto enough to give him a million-dollar boat with enough power to ditch me anytime he wanted. Further complicating things was my desire to run directly from Puerto Vallarta to Cabo San Lucas, a trip of over three hundred miles. Heading up the coast to Mazatlan and shooting straight across would shave almost a hundred miles off the crossing, but I'd had enough of Mexico, and there was still the passport issue if a nosy agent boarded us. It was better to keep a low profile, and staying to open water would do that. There was no choice except to tow the *Nai'a* to Cabo and dock her there while we took the *Dorado* back. I wanted her closer than the mainland. After collecting the larger bounty, I could fly back and retrieve her.

Something finally went as planned and we entered the harbor at daybreak. There was plenty of activity with the local fishing fleet going out for the day to allow our arrival to go unnoticed. Roberto dropped me at the fuel dock. I left him with enough from Gerardo's money to fill the tanks and with instructions to meet me just outside the river inlet. This was as far as I planned on letting him out of my sight. Marcella and the cash were another matter. With the messenger bag slung over my shoulder, the two of us left the marina and walked as quickly as we could without attracting attention to ourselves toward the river and the *Nai'a*. To my relief, she was where we had left her.

I waded out, climbed aboard, and stashed the bag in the cabin. Marcella came over the transom right after me, and we quickly pulled anchor and motored to the mouth of the river. Just as we were about to set the anchor and wait, I saw a stainless tower moving toward us from the direction of the gas dock. The hull was screened by land, but the boat quickly rounded the bend, and there was Roberto waving to us from the bridge of the *Dorado*. Together we motored to the turning basin, where I slowed to let him pass. Just as he came alongside, I saw the towline come across our bow and left the helm to secure it to the forward cleat. Taking in the line, I had Marcella idle to the stern of the larger boat. She stopped just short of the swim platform, and I helped her aboard the sportfisher. After a last check of the towline, I followed and signaled Roberto to head out of the harbor.

Finally, after adjusting the towline, I sat against the gunwale and breathed. So far, so good. I had both boats and open water ahead. The time passed slowly, and I started getting nervous when the afternoon breeze kicked up. The *Nai'a* was not an easy tow, and the windblown waves only made it worse. I had her three waves back, with both boats cresting the waves at the same time, but the line required constant attention to keep her synchronized with the larger boat.

We had all been together through the day, but around sunset, with twenty hours of travel ahead of us, I split the watch with Roberto. We were burning fuel at almost twice the normal rate, and we were stuck traveling at twelve knots, the maximum hull speed of the sailboat. Any faster would cause her to porpoise through the water, making her even harder to tow and increasing our fuel consumption.

* * *

It had been a tense but uneventful night. Towing in open water was difficult during the day—in the dark it was multiple times worse. According to the GPS, we still had another hundred miles to go, and by my calculations we would reach the southern tip of the peninsula in about eight hours. The *Nai'a* still bobbed obediently behind us, and I started to relax as the sun rose. Weather permitting, we would anchor off Cabo that night, meet up with Gerardo in the morning, and I would be on my way to San Diego to collect the bounty on the *Dorado*.

Marcella had been quiet and withdrawn overnight. She had spent most of the hours below. We were all exhausted from the last few days, and I wrote it off to that, until Roberto came up to the bridge to relieve me.

"How long have you and the *señorita* been together?" he asked.

At first I took it as a compliment of how well we worked together, but I still couldn't read him. "Just this week," I said, fishing for information.

"Maybe I should tell you something," he said.

I looked at him, encouraging him to talk.

"Her phone was on the counter. I didn't want to look, but the screen lit up and there was a message."

"When was that?" I asked.

"Just before we left Puerto Vallarta. There are people upset with her and looking for her," he said, and headed down the ladder for his break.

I had known something was going on. This only confirmed it. It had been hard enough to put her from my mind during the last few days. Now, with the boredom of the crossing, she was all I could think about—and I was confused to the point that I knew any decision I made would be suspect. Just as I thought it, she appeared on the bridge.

"Good morning," she said, pulling her arms over her head and stretching.

Of course, this only pulled her loose shirt tight against her breasts. "Hey," I said, trying to concentrate on the instruments.

"What's the plan?" she asked, sitting next to me so our bare legs touched.

"Should be in Cabo tonight. When we get close, can you get ahold of your sister and see if we can meet up in the morning?"

A worried look came over her face. She tried to hide it with a smile. "Sure. How about some breakfast?" she asked.

"That would be great," I said, watching her descend the stairs.

I knew the history between the two sisters now and understood some of Marcella's resentment, but not her actions.

They were from a different culture, one very distant from the way I was raised, and that might explain some of it. And she really hadn't jeopardized her sister; just delayed her rescue, I rationalized. Roberto had confirmed she was in some kind of trouble, and I realized she had lost her bets. Maybe Gerardo would pay them. I had thought long and hard on it and still had not reached a decision on what I would do if she wanted to come north with me. I still had that "yes" problem, and in my heart I knew myself, and I wouldn't or couldn't say no.

Trying to put that aside, I looked back at the *Nai'a* plowing behind us, then turned to the GPS. Eighty miles to go.

* * *

We made landfall at five. The weather was calm and the seas were down, making it safe to anchor outside the harbor. Roberto took control of the *Dorado*, and I waited on deck to handle the *Nai'a*. He slowed until the momentum of the sailboat brought her alongside. I hauled the towline in and, with every fender out, Marcella and I brought the two boats together. Just as we secured her, I heard the anchor drop. Roberto looked down to make sure we were clear before backing down to set the hook. A few minutes later, the boats swung together and settled in to the motion of the seas.

"You have enough scope out?" I yelled up, questioning how much line he had out.

"*Si*. Over two hundred feet."

Anchored in thirty feet of water, that was close to a seven-to-one ratio, and in these conditions plenty of protection. I went aboard the *Nai'a* to remove my personal belongings and ready her for docking. Marcella came aboard with me to help.

Compared to the luxury of the *Dorado*, it was tight quarters in the cabin, and we brushed against each other several times while gathering our belongings, each time sending an electric shock up my spine. Finally I couldn't help myself and we found ourselves entangled on the forward V berth.

Afterward we lay together quietly, neither wanting to ask what our future held. Marcella got up to use the head. As always, I couldn't take my eyes off her, and with her shape illuminated in the late afternoon light, I saw her freeze. It was less than a second, but she had seen something. Waiting until she was in the small bathroom, I raised myself on an elbow and looked out into the galley. In the dim light I could see the bag of money sitting on the settee.

Chapter 30

Anyone would have stopped and stared at a bag with a million dollars, I rationalized, almost believing myself. As usual, she quickly redirected my concern when she came out of the head and lay next to me. We lay together talking about nothing when I noticed the motion of the boat increase. At first I thought it was the wake from a passing boat, then maybe another. When it didn't stop after a minute, I got up and looked out the hatch. The wind had kicked up.

Afternoon wind was a common occurrence and nothing to be concerned about in itself, except the boats were rafted together with only the four fenders separating them. This might have been okay if the hulls were similar. But in this case they didn't match well at all, and I could already feel the rub rail of the larger sportfisher slamming against the deck of the sailboat.

"We need to split the boats," I said, pulling on my board shorts and moving toward the deck. I called out to Roberto on the flybridge of the *Dorado* and he agreed. There was too much wind to remain rafted together. We would have to anchor separately. Another wave unbalanced me and I moved forward to set the anchor. It would be easier to move the more maneuverable sportfisher.

"What's going on?" Marcella asked from the companionway as another wave lifted us.

"Going to move," I called back, releasing the ties on the hook but pausing before I threw it. Roberto saw what I was doing and slid down the stairs, landing on the deck of the *Dorado*. "Go ahead and take the bags across," I told Marcella.

The decks were moving up and down, making an easy crossing seem impossible. I changed course and refastened the ties, leaving the anchor in its compartment.

"I don't know," she said, tossing the backpack and duffel onto the deck and looking warily at the motion of the two boats.

"I'm thinking we should head into the harbor and take a slip," I said, starting to think ahead. My plan was to leave the *Nai'a* here anyway. Why risk a night anchored in building seas with what I already knew was insufficient ground tackle? There was a look in her eye that I couldn't place, but I was quickly distracted when another wave lifted us and slammed us against the hull of the *Dorado*.

"We are going to head in and grab a slip. I can get a water taxi to take us back out," I called over to Roberto. Moving to the helm, I started the engine. "Let her go," I yelled to Marcella.

She undid the lines, allowing the boats to drift apart, but they were dangerously close. Pushing the throttle forward, I steered straight toward land, hoping I would clear the sportfisher and still have room to turn before hitting bottom. There was no other choice. The *Nai'a* didn't have enough power to back away with any kind of control in these seas.

Slowly the two boats slid apart. Roberto was back on the bridge of the *Dorado*. There was nothing he could do but watch. Another wave lifted us, but this time I was able to use it to our advantage and turned the wheel to starboard, placing us beam toward the swells. We were clear of the *Dorado* now and parallel with the beach. Pushing the throttle down, using every ounce of power the engine had, we moved away from the larger boat. But now the swells were pushing us toward the beach. I turned the wheel hard to starboard again and heard the propeller dig in. The bow swung around and we moved away from land.

The harbor was less than a mile away, and within a few minutes we entered the breakwater. "Can you call the dock master and get us a slip?" I asked Marcella, holding up the VHF microphone. I knew they spoke English, but I figured if there were questions it would be easier for her to handle in Spanish. "Tell them we need to leave the boat for a month."

We idled through the busy port, passing the dock where I had my first run-in with Chuy. We were assigned an out-of-the-way berth on F dock, near the back of the harbor. Facing the bow out, I turned with my butt to the wheel and drove us backward into the slip. Several young boys were waiting with lines to help. In a few minutes, we were secure and I took a deep breath.

"Can we get something to eat?" Marcella asked.

I looked around at the busy streets and felt my stomach grumble. "Sure. Be right there," I said, going below. The bag of money was still there, and I grabbed a few rolls of bills, peeling off a hundred to tip the boys. They would have eagerly taken a five, but this was their lucky day. I closed the bag and looked around for a hiding place. I settled on the compartment under the V berth. Lifting the seat cushion off, I opened the hatch and dropped the bag in. Turning to move away, I saw Marcella move away from the opening. With the rolls of bills jammed in my pockets, I climbed the short ladder to the deck.

I helped her off the boat and gave the bill to the boys. They were soon our tour guides, walking with us down the dock and onto the street. At the end of the dock we turned right and headed toward a cantina. It felt weird sitting at a table in an air-conditioned restaurant after being at sea for several weeks. And across from me was Marcella. I couldn't help but notice the looks from the other tables and smiled.

"This is like out first date," I said.

"We should celebrate," she said. "Maybe we can stay in a hotel tonight. There's not much privacy on the boat." She winked.

I melted and ordered two of the jumbo top-shelf Cadillac, throw everything you've got in it, Margaritas. We toasted, finished those, and ordered two more with our dinner. Besides the fish I caught, we hadn't had a real meal in days. I polished off the second drink, ordering another to wash down the rest of my food. I slowed down, realizing she was looking at me, still sipping her second drink.

"Go ahead. You deserve it," she said, toasting me.

I knew the alcohol was affecting me, but I was powerless to stop. I was basking in the glow of victory, and there was a beautiful woman sitting across from me. Finishing the food, I ordered one more drink, and maybe another after that, as we sat there quietly watching the tourists walk by.

* * *

The sun hit my face and I struggled to open my eyes. With my head pounding, I lifted one lid and saw the room in full daylight. It took me a minute to piece together where I was, but then it came back to me and I smiled. It had been a memorable night. Reaching across the bed, I found it empty and rose slowly looking for Marcella. I fought off a wave of nausea, cursing myself for the last drink, and looked around the room. It was empty. I lay back down, thinking she had gone for coffee, and slowly I tried to wake up.

After about fifteen minutes, I rose, wondering where she was. I got up and dressed. After splashing water on my face, I left the room and headed toward the docks. The boys from last night quickly found me and started to follow. As we approached the dock, I scanned the horizon for the mast of the *Nai'a*, but it was like looking for a single tree in a forest, impossible to tell one from the other at this distance.

"The *señorita?*" I asked the boys, trying to find some Spanish to communicate.

"*Si,*" one of them answered. "She go. We help her, and she says to find you for a tip," he said proudly in broken English.

I took off at a run with the boys close on my heels, not stopping until I reached the empty slip.

"Shit," I said. They giggled. Ignoring them. I searched for a water taxi, finding one at the next pier. I ran down the dock to the street, turned and hailed the driver. The boys were still right behind me, laughing and enjoying what they thought was an adventure. Reaching into my pocket, I was relieved to find the cash I had stashed there and peeled off a bill. They took it and ran toward town.

"*Vamanos,*" I yelled to the driver. He had seen the wad of bills and quickly tossed the line and accelerated. "Out of the harbor." I motioned toward the inlet, not knowing how much English he had. I was climbing out of my skin as we left the breakwater behind and headed toward Lovers Beach, where I hoped the *Dorado* was still anchored. For a frantic moment, I couldn't see the boat, until finally the tower came into view and I urged the driver to go faster.

We reached the sportfisher and I peeled a bill off the pile and handed it to the man. Roberto was waiting, clearly unsure of what was going on. "Have you seen the sailboat?" I yelled to him, waiting impatiently for the water taxi to maneuver close enough to the sportfisher for me to board.

"No." He looked at me like he had done something wrong.

"Never mind. We have to go," I said, jumping across the void to the deck. He was already up the ladder and I joined him on the flybridge. A long minute later, the anchor was up and we were underway.

"Where to?" he asked. "And the *señorita?*"

I scanned the horizon, trying to reach through the cobwebs in my head and figure out what had happened. It didn't take a rocket scientist. Marcella had taken the sailboat and damned near a million dollars. I had seen all the warning signs and ignored them. Without answering, I pointed north, up the coast. She might have played me for the boat and the money, but I knew sailors, and although she had caught on quickly, she was a novice. There was no faking that. She wouldn't risk an open water crossing. If I were her, I would find the easiest port I could make, hoping we misjudged her route. I pointed north and felt the vibration of the engines beneath me. With our power, even if she was more experienced than I thought, we would catch her in an hour.

Chapter 31

Sensing my urgency, Roberto pushed the boat hard. Just beyond the long beach I had anchored off before, I saw a mast bobbing in the waves. In another minute, we were close enough to see that she was running under power, and I saw the first sign of her inexperience. Not understanding the effect of the current, she was dangerously close to the rocks and was probably wondering why the wheel was fighting her as she tried to move away.

"Stay back," I told Roberto. I didn't want to spook her until I had a plan. We paced her, leaving enough sea room between us that I doubted she noticed us.

"She's in trouble," Roberto said.

I saw it too. She was trying to put the sails up. As mad as I was, I found myself rooting for her. Maybe so we didn't lose the boat and cash, or maybe because I had taught her. With the bow into the wind, she was on the foredeck and I could see the main come up. With the autopilot on, the boat was in irons, allowing her to reach the cockpit.

Then I saw the course change, and there was nothing I could do. "Hurry," I yelled to Roberto.

It was like the boat pulled itself from her grasp. The wind filled the sail, healing her over to port. I saw the jib start to unfurl and knew it was too late. Adding more canvas would put her on the rocks. Instead of turning to starboard and deeper water to bring the sails up and then tack back, she had continued on her course, and with the wind and current running together the sails only pushed her faster toward the rocks.

The sportfisher planed out, running at her maximum speed toward the sailboat. We were close enough that I could see the panic in her eyes. I couldn't be sure whether it was the recognition that we had caught her, or the rocks, now only twenty feet from her bow. Still a hundred yards off her stern, there was nothing we could do. Roberto knew it too, and slowed.

Together we watched the bow strike. The boat seemed to stay in place, and I thought I saw a pleading look in her eyes as it slowly turned, the rock tearing across her starboard side. Within seconds the boat foundered. The sail was flat in the water, at least for a moment keeping her afloat, but I knew once a wave filled the canvas it would act as an anchor and take the boat quickly to the bottom.

"We have to help her," I yelled, leaving Roberto at the controls and jumping down to the deck. He backed down on the sailboat, but it was too late. Desperately I scanned the water, looking for Marcella. I sat mesmerized for a few seconds. There was nothing I could do except watch the boat sink in the gin-clear water. It stopped, the sail still visible in the water, and I saw a stream of bubbles rise to the surface. She was on the bottom.

"How deep is it?" I yelled up.

"Sixty feet," Roberto called down. He bumped the engine into forward again, struggling to keep us over the site. "Should we anchor?"

I thought for a second about the twenty-seven ways this could go badly and decided against it. "I'll throw the buoy instead," I answered, reaching under the gunwale and tossing the weighted float over the side. Opening the fish locker, I reached for the snorkeling gear I had found on an earlier inspection. Figuring she had been in the water for over a minute already, I snugged the mask over my face, pushed the snorkel out of the way, and donned the fins. After pulling the straps tight, I started to breathe deeply. More of a scuba diver, I had played around with free diving, but was constantly frustrated by my lack of breath-holding ability. Where most good divers could stay down for three minutes, if I broke sixty seconds, it was a good effort.

Pulling in hard, I sucked air in for a count of eight, held for a few seconds, and released it under pressure. Four times I repeated the cycle before I slid over the side. Putting the snorkel in my mouth, I took several more breaths while trying to get directly above the wreck. I finned above the site, released the last breath and spit the snorkel from my mouth. My body pivoted, and with my hands in front and one knee bent to my chest I jackknifed into the water. Reaching ahead of me, I pulled two hard breaststrokes and then started using my legs. I had never been below thirty feet, having washed out of the free-diving course a friend in the Keys had taught, but I knew when I felt the pressure force me to slow and clear my ears that I had exceeded that mark.

The wreck was only feet from me when I felt the burning in my lungs and I convulsed. I knew I passed the minute mark. Ignoring the uncomfortable sensation, I kicked toward the deck of the boat and found no sign of Marcella. Estimating that she had been down for almost five minutes now, I finned myself into the companionway. Convulsing again, I tried to push the fear from my mind and pulled myself inside. If she were there, I had to get her now. Having to surface for another breath would take minutes that she didn't have. A school of small fish swam past my facemask as I scanned the galley. There was still no sign of her. I was feeling lightheaded and knew I had only seconds left. With one hard kick I found myself in the V berth, staring into her lifeless eyes.

There was no question that she was gone, and I turned to exit when my fin snagged on something. I spun. Panicking, I released the remaining air in my lungs and yanked off the fin. I was just about to turn to surface when I saw what had happened. Marcella's lifeless hand was tangled around the strap of the messenger bag, which must have stuck in the compartment where I had stashed it. I grabbed for it, and jamming my finless foot against the deck, tore it loose.

I spun, disoriented, until the light from the companionway hit me and I kicked as hard as I could toward freedom. With one fin and the bag behind me, I was moving too slowly. The surface was visible, but so had the bottom been when I was on the boat. I gagged again, this time swallowing a mouthful of water.

* * *

When I came to, I found myself in the cockpit of the *Dorado* with Roberto hovering over me. I lifted my head. "We gotta go," was all I could say before I dropped back to the deck. His shadow moved from my face, and a few seconds later I felt the big diesels throttle up and the boat move out.

Slowly I got to my feet, not sure how long I had been out. We were up on plane, moving fast, and I looked toward the land on our starboard side. Still disoriented, I slid open the salon door and entered the cabin. Stepping over the bag sitting in a puddle in the middle of the floor, I went to the galley and grabbed a bottle of water. With a hand braced against the counter, I drank the whole thing, tossed the bottle, and grabbed another. I left the bag where it was and went up to the bridge.

"You okay, *jefe*?" Roberto asked. "I was scared for you there."

I nodded and looked at the chart plotter. It showed us heading west around the southern tip of the peninsula. "Good job," I said. He had done exactly the right thing. "Did anyone see us?" I asked.

"No. It was too early for the snorkel boats," he said.

I nodded and sat in the chair next to him, feeling very alive with the breeze blowing through my hair. The *Nai'a* and Marcella were gone, but I had little feeling for either right now. She had used me, and ditched me at the end. Now I was mad at myself for being that much of a fool and not trusting my instincts. The *Nai'a* and I had been through a lot, but in the big picture, with the *Dorado* now in our control, this would be the trip I needed to start my own business.

And there were close to a million soaked dollars on the floor of the cabin. There was no question, I would give it back, but for now, it was insurance that we would make it back to San Diego. Exhausted, I set the water bottle in the cup holder, leaned back and closed my eyes.

Chapter 32

I had to admit that taking a sportfisher the size of the *Dorado* up the Pacific Coast of Baja was an unexpected bonus. The ten-day trip, beating into the wind from Cabo to San Diego in a sailboat, turned into a two-day easy ride. We made one stop in Turtle Bay, a little more than halfway up the coast, to refuel, carefully planning on entering the harbor at dawn, just after the marina opened and before the customs agent was likely to have crawled out of bed. Before he would have finished his coffee, we had fueled and exited the harbor.

I breathed a sigh of relief when the sun went down and the chart plotter showed we had entered US waters. Instead of heading north to San Diego, I pushed the wheel to port and set a northwesterly course. Powering up the coast would be a red flag to the US immigration officials, so we took a slight detour to and dragged some baits around San Clemente Island. Now with several nice tuna aboard, we ran the seventy-five miles straight east to San Diego, looking like every other fishing charter.

We entered the dock and I paid for a slip, then called Salvage Solutions to arrange the turnover of the vessel. By tomorrow morning I would be homeless, but with a pocketful of money.

At the marina office, I had picked up a boat trader magazine and sat on the flybridge looking for that pennies-on-the-dollar find I had dreamed of.

"Will?" I heard a woman call up.

I looked down and jumped as if I had seen a ghost. Marisa stood by the boat wearing a wide-brimmed hat similar to the one I had first seen Marcella wearing. I quickly recovered and saw Gerardo come up beside her.

I climbed down and helped her aboard. Gerardo easily jumped across. We sat outside, drinking beer and reminiscing about Marcella, each expressing our feelings. Generally, we agreed, she had a good heart but had been led astray.

After we finished the beers, Gerardo and I went inside to settle up. He graciously allowed the missing money to go toward expenses and took the remainder. I said goodbye to the couple and greeted Roberto, who had been out looking for work.

"Any luck?" I asked.

"*Si*. I have two offers to be a mate on fishing charters. It is something I have not done for years, but a place to start over," he said.

"Not to worry. You're a good captain. You'll move up fast enough."

We talked over another beer and watched the sun set. He went below to get some sleep for his first day of work tomorrow, and I sat alone, drinking another beer and enjoying the quiet. Tomorrow was going to be a big day.

Thanks For Reading

For more information please check out my web page:
https://stevenbeckerauthor.com/

Or follow me on Facebook:
https://www.facebook.com/stevenbecker.books/

Made in the USA
Monee, IL
07 July 2023

38792923R00109